ALL HE TAKES

(A Vivian Fox Suspense Thriller —Book 1)

Ella Swift

Ella Swift

Ella Swift is author of the VIVIAN FOX suspense thriller series, comprising five books (and counting); PEYTON RISK mystery series, comprising five books (and counting); and of the new COOPER TRACE mystery series, comprising five books (and counting).

An avid reader and lifelong fan of the mystery and thriller genres, Ella loves to hear from you, so please feel free to visit ellaswiftauthor.com to learn more and stay in touch.

ISBN: 978-1-0943-9769-6

BOOKS BY ELLA SWIFT

PEYTON RISK MYSTERY SERIES
WHAT'S HIS (Book #1)
WHAT'S LEFT (Book #2)
WHAT'S WISHED (Book #3)
WHAT'S GONE (Book #4)
WHAT'S MINE (Book #5)

COOPER TRACE MYSTERY SERIES
SHATTERED MIND (Book #1)
SHATTERED LIFE (Book #2)
SHATTERED HOPE (Book #3)
SHATTERED DREAM (Book #4)
SHATTERED FATE (Book #5)

VIVIAN FOX MYSTERY SERIES
ALL HE TAKES (Book #1)
ALL HE HIDES (Book #2)
ALL HE COVETS (Book #3)
ALL HE NEEDS (Book #4)
ALL HE DESTROYS (Book #5)

PROLOGUE

Sarah stumbled out into the New York City night, her high heels clicking unevenly against the pavement. She had to hold herself up against the door of the bar for a moment, making sure she was going to be able to walk. She'd had a bit too much to drink whether she wanted to admit it or not.

Around her, the city was ablaze with life, though given the late hour it wasn't quite as alive as it usually was. Not on a Tuesday night, anyway. Still, neon signs blinked in a frenzied dance of colors half a block over. Taxis honked incessantly, their yellow bodies weaving through traffic like frantic bees. Above, the skyscrapers were jagged silhouettes against a sky that never truly darkened, stars obscured by the perpetual glow of the city that never slept.

Sarah clutched her purse tighter under her arm, aware of just how badly off her equilibrium was. Her mind was a blur, her thoughts as tangled as the people spilling from bars and clubs onto the sidewalks. She should book an Uber, she thought, but pride and a desire to shake off the cobwebs of too many cocktails spurred her on.

"Just five blocks," she muttered to herself, trying to steady her spinning world with the promise of a short walk home. "Walk it off…"

So that's what she decided to do. On slightly wobbly legs, she started venturing toward her apartment building.

"Hey there," came a voice, smooth as silk but with a predatory edge that cut through her inebriated haze. A man she'd seen in the bar sidled up to her, coming out of nowhere like some horny ghost. He had watched her in the bar, laughter easy on his lips, but now, outside, he seemed more imposing. His hand brushed against her arm, his touch sending an unwelcome shiver down her spine.

"Let me walk you home," he offered. It was obvious that he was drunk, too, his words slurred slightly. His eyes were hazy as well, but it did little to disguise the lust there.

"I'm fine," Sarah replied, her voice firmer than she felt. "It's just up the street." She tried to step around him, but he shifted to block her path, his presence suddenly suffocating.

"Come on, don't be like that," he pressed, his flirtation now a mask barely concealing frustration. "You were all charry in the bar."

"Because I knew I could leave whenever I liked."

Being hit on was nothing new to her. And, to her credit, she's made quite the art form of letting men down gently. But if this guy kept pressing, she didn't think there would be anything gentle about how to she eventually reacted.

No, really," she pressed. "I want to walk. I need some air." With a practiced wriggle that came from years of bar-hopping, she managed to move past him.

"Your loss," he called after her, his voice carrying a note of wounded ego.

She smiled at the sound of it. *Good.*

Relief flooded Sarah as she put distance between them, the encounter leaving her skin prickling with unease. She quickened her pace, the city's rhythmic pulse now a backdrop to her own racing heartbeat.

Maybe it was time to stop going out so late, of drinking so much. She considered herself to be still young, just thirty-two years old, and finally making a name for herself at work. It was time to stop worrying about the next party or the next happy hour; instead, it was time to put her attention toward that corner office that awaited her, the glass walls, the skyline view — the reward for years of relentless drive. She'd been told in no uncertain terms that it was hers if she wanted it. She just needed to give a bit extra at work, a bit more focus.

Her mind raced through campaign strategies and client meetings. She'd have a hell of a headache tomorrow, and she had no one but herself to blame. Yeah…it was definitely time for a course-correction.

The city's night-song dulled to a whisper as she turned onto a quieter street, where the buildings pressed closer together. Peering ahead, she could see the upper portion of the roof of her building. And somehow, it seemed she *had* sobered up a bit—whether from the thoughts of her future or the walk itself, she wasn't certain.

As she headed towards home, her ears caught a thread of conversation to her right. Men's voices, hushed and coarse, sliced through the quiet. They were close, too close, their whispers laced with the sharp edge of anger and urgency. Sarah slowed her steps, instinctively drawing her coat tighter around her.

Her apartment was just ahead, about a block and a half. Yet, even as she yearned for the comfort of home, curiosity tugged at her. Who were these men, and what were they trying to be so secretive about? Recalling the man who's tried picking her up less than fifteen minutes ago, her thoughts turned to other helpless women and how predatory men did everything they could to take advantage. What if that was what she was hearing, and she simply walked away?

A sense of foreboding crept over her, a silent alarm that buzzed at the edges of her consciousness.

She chanced a discreet glance toward the source of the whispers, careful not to betray her attention. Nothing seemed amiss, just the ordinary play of light and shadow along the streets. Sarah shook her head, berating herself for letting the night's earlier encounter fray her nerves.

But then there was movement. Two shadows emerged from the yawning doorway of a nondescript brownstone, their forms swallowed by the inkiness of the night. Sarah stopped mid-stride, her gaze locked onto the figures. They were both dressed in black from head to toe, faces obscured by ski masks that left only their eyes exposed. They moved with a fluidity that was almost spectral, their steps silent on the pavement, bodies tensed like snakes giving a warning.

Sarah's heart skipped a beat. The promotion, the bar, the unwanted advances—all of it evaporated as one of the men locked eyes with her. One of them, bulkier than the other, carried what appeared to be a duffel bag, its contents hidden but undoubtedly significant given the care with which he cradled it in his arms.

Her heartbeat continued to flutter as she realized that she had stumbled across something clandestine, something illicit.

And with this realization, one of the men turned in her direction. For a blood-curdling moment, their eyes locked.

Panic clawed at her insides, urging her to turn, to run. *Yeah, right,* she thought. *Run while drunk and wearing these heels?*

Still, she did attempt to retreat, to get home as quickly as possible. She pivoted on unsteady heels, her legs a blend of lead and jelly as she quickened her pace.

She had barely covered a few yards when a sudden pressure clamped around her arm, iron-strong and unforgiving. In that moment, time contracted, the bustling cityscape narrowing to the vice-like grip that anchored her to the spot.

She raised her free arm to strike at whoever had grabbed her at the very same moment she opened her mouth to scream for help. But before she could do either, she was wrenched backward. A fist buried itself in her abdomen, the force blunt and unexpected. Air whooshed from her lungs, her scream dissolving into a helpless gasp. She doubled over instinctively, pain radiating through her core.

Her captor grabbed the fabric of her coat as he hauled her half-stumbling, half-dragged toward a nondescript van parked at the curb. Its back doors yawned open like the maw of some great beast. The interior was shrouded in darkness. The other masked figure had already slipped inside, waiting.

Sarah's mind raced. She knew she needed to scream, to call for help, but her breaths came in shallow, ragged pulls that made her head spin even more than the alcohol still rampaging through her.

As they neared the van, the world tilted dangerously, her perspective narrowing until there was nothing but the cold grasp of her captor…and the waiting maw of the van.

"Please," she managed to whisper.

But her plea went unheeded; the only response was the tightening of the man's grip and the looming shadow of the van as she was shoved inside.

CHAPTER ONE

Vivian Fox's boots whispered across the polished floor, her shadow a fleeting ghost in the dim light of the hallway. The museum was still and quiet around her, the only sound coming from the subtle hum of air conditioning. The building itself was quite simple and basic, but the priceless artifacts contained under the roof gave the space a feeling of importance and antiquity.

It wasn't the smallest museum Vivian had broken into, but it was a close contender. The sleepy little museum, located just a bit off the edge of the University of Virginia in Charlottesville, held a quaint colonial charm. But it was also about to lose a treasure that had once bristled under the might of the Spanish Armada.

Her breath steady, Vivian moved with purpose, the weight of her compact duffel bag a reassuring presence at her side. She navigated the labyrinth of displays and plaques, each step taking her closer to the reason she was here. There was a certain thrill to this, a rush of adrenaline she found nowhere else…that she doubted *anyone* ever felt unless they, too, were a professional thief.

When she came to the room where her target was located, she slowed her step. The golden gleam of the coins beckoned from the end of the corridor, barely shining in the soft light of the museum's after-hours ambience. Vivian could almost feel the weight of the coins in her palm, the cool metal speaking volumes of centuries passed. They were pieces of history, soon to be spirited away into the hands of someone who would hoard them rather than share their story.

That particular part of her job did bother her from time to time, but the pay often squashed that tiny, moral concern. It was a job—just another job—but one that came with the satisfaction of outsmarting systems designed to be foolproof.

She had done her part well. An hour earlier, tucked away in the shadows a block from the museum, she'd pulled up the inner-workings of the museum's security system via a portable hard drive provided by her client. In the back of a small van, she'd studied lines of code as she'd disabled alarms and blinded cameras. The security system had folded effortlessly under her expertise, a testament to years of honing her craft. It had seemed too easy, but Vivian wasn't one to question good fortune.

This was no smash-and-grab; it was artistry, a game of wits played on a field of both technology and darkness. There was no clanging of breached doors or flashing lights on patrol cars to worry about—she'd made sure of that. Vivian prided herself on being a ghost; it was a talent that had some of the world's most powerful and mysterious people seeking her out for jobs just like this one.

The display case loomed ahead, unassuming yet holding riches that empires had bled for. A small smile flirted with the edges of her lips. Everything was going according to plan, every contingency accounted for. She thought she may even set a new record tonight—in and out in under ninety seconds.

The glass case before her was the size of a shoebox, the clear walls guarding its treasure. She slipped her slender, gloved fingers into her jacket pocket and retrieved a small, leather-bound kit. Unfolding it on the floor, the delicate array of picks and tension wrenches winked under the muted lights.

She chose her tools quickly, knowing their shapes and abilities intimately. She selected the right tools for the job, tools so well-designed that the lock she was about to pick would show no signs of having been tampered with. The box that she'd be leaving empty, however, was another story completely.

As the tumblers fell into place, a quiet satisfaction hummed through her veins. Each click was like music to her, like the applause of an unseen crowd. *Good job,* they seemed to say.

With a final click, the case opened.

She took a moment to admire the coins before plucking them out of the glass container. They were beautiful and relics of history, but they were not for her. They were destined for the private collection of a man whose obsession with Spanish gold had filled his vaults yet emptied his soul. A millionaire, yes, but a prisoner to his own desires…just like most of her clients.

Her client had provided access to the security system and even the museum network the coins were in. All told, Vivian had spent roughly five hours on this job—staking out the museum during opening hours, researching the security system and then disabling it, and now these few minutes spent on the actual theft itself.

Five hours, and she was going to net a cool eighty thousand dollars when all was said and done.

Vivian slipped a velvet pouch from her duffel bag, each movement deliberate and practiced. One by one, she transferred the coins—all twelve of them, having been rescued from the ocean floor twenty years ago. They spoke of conquests and kings, of storms at sea and the darkness beneath the waves. And Vivian felt proud to be holding them.

The pouch now heavy with its precious cargo, she tucked it securely into her bag. With the job done, she immediately turned back the way she had come, ready to melt back into the shadows. She strode back through the quiet, her footsteps making no noise at all, her body light and agile.

She left the room and turned the corner to head back toward the exit. She'd taken just a single step when she saw the three men standing halfway down the hall. They were dressed in basic police uniforms, and though all three were armed, none of them had their sidearms drawn.

Her mind raced, thoughts tangling like the wires she had so carefully navigated through in the security system. She'd knocked the security out and only two people on the face of the planet knew she was here. Her thoughts turned to the only possible answer: she'd been set-up.

But why?

Her breath quickened, but not from fear. It was rage that tightened her chest. They had underestimated her if they thought she'd be an easy catch.

She pivoted, her previous exit now a trap. The back-up route beckoned, a narrow passage between ancient artifacts and dusty shadows to her right. Vivian dashed towards it, her duffel bag snug against her side, the coins within a heavy reminder of the job half-done.

As she rounded a corner, the sharp scent of gun oil hit her nostrils, a metallic tang in the air. There, blocking her way, stood two more policemen. This duo *did* have their weapons drawn and leveled at her.

"Freeze!" the officer on the right commanded. His voice, firm and unyielding, suggested no discussion would follow.

But Vivian had faced down more than uniformed men with guns before. She had a bit of government training in the area, as well as over twenty years of kickboxing, Brazilian Jiu-Jitsu, and Muay Thai training. She assessed their positioning, adapted her plan in the span of a heartbeat, and prepared to act.

"Easy there," Vivian said. Her voice was steady and almost conversational despite the adrenaline coursing through her veins. "Let's not do anything hasty."

"Put the bag down and put your hands where we can see them," the second officer barked, stepping closer, the muzzle of his gun an unblinking eye. Vivian was also aware of the other three cops, likely coming to the corner behind her within just another few seconds.

That was when Vivian made her choice. With a fluid movement born of desperation and honed skill, she lunged to one side, her action a blur designed to confuse and disorient.. She feinted left, then spun right, her heel connecting with the lead officer's wrist. The gun clattered to the tile floor, its metallic clang ridiculously loud in the museum's night-time silence.

The other officer lunged, only for Vivian to duck and weave through the gap his bulk created. In his lunging, Vivian deduced that whoever had sent them had instructed them not to shoot her. That simple knowledge gave her a huge advantage in the fight.

She darted past artifacts and dimly lit exhibits that blurred into indistinct shapes, her breath a ragged counterpoint to her footfalls. Shadows clung to the edges of the museum halls, offering up possible hiding spots.

"Stop her!"

The shout barely registered as she burst through a service door, her backup route a darkened promise of escape. But fate, it seemed, had other plans. Two more officers stepped from the shadows, their outlines solidifying like nightmares given form.

"End of the line, Fox," one of these officers said. There was a taser in his hand, its electric hum somehow more alarming that the guns the other officers had held. Maybe they'd been told not to *shoot* her. But being tased was a completely different thing.

Vivian's body moved on instinct. She launched herself at the nearest threat, her elbow swinging in a vicious arc. It connected solidly with the face of the first cop, clearly taken by surprise at her speed and fluidity. She barely heard him strike the wall following her attack and then crumple to the floor.

But by the time she was out of this attack, the other officer had already acted. He'd fired off the taser, his face a mask of determination.

Pain erupted through Vivian, fierce and blinding. Her muscles seized, uncontrollable, as thousands of volts passed through her. Vivian hit the ground hard, the impact jarring, the world tilting sideways in a disorienting kaleidoscope. She’d never been tased before and had no idea just how badly it hurt. Even when the initial jolt was over, the pain radiated through her.

She heard the cops murmuring, heard the drum-like pattern of footfalls as all of the cops converged to the one spot where she’d fallen.

Cuffs closed around her wrists. It was a sound and feeling she'd heard before, but it seemed more final this time. Vivian lay there, gasping on the cold floor. a stark contrast to the heat of her skin. The scent of ozone lingered in her nostrils from the jolt that had taken her down.

Her vision swam, the once precise lines of the museum warping. As consciousness threatened to slip away, Vivian's last coherent thought was bitter, edged with anger.

Who had turned the tables on her?

CHAPTER TWO

Vivian's muscles still twitched as two burly officers hoisted her up and carried her with a speed that belied their size. She blinked hard, trying to clear the fog of disorientation. Her hands were cuffed behind her back, limiting any attempt at struggle. One moment they were in the darkened museum halls and the next, the cool night air slapped at her face.

The fresh air and coolness of the night seemed to bring her around a bit. Her senses cleared just enough for her to become aware of the white van parked behind the museum. She was being taken to the van, the back door opened like an unhinged jaw just waiting for her.

“Whatsit…” she said, struggling to get control of herself. Good Lord, that shock had taken just about all of her energy right out of her.

She was lifted completely off the ground and fed into the back of the van. The interior was softly lit by faint, golden light. She expected to be simply tossed onto the floor but was surprised when gentle hands actually made sure she was sitting up. As her vision began to swim into focus, she started to see the shapes of what looked like couches—but of course, that made no sense. She was in the back of a van, after all.

She heard a deep male voice ask: “We good?”

She didn’t hear an answer, but she *did* hear the back doors of the van. They slammed shut with an ominous thud. Vivian expelled a breath she didn’t realize she’d been holding. Right away, she heard an engine come to life and then the van was moving.

She winced as one last little flicker of pain tore through her. She blinked her eyes rapidly, as if willing her vision to come back to full force. It wasn’t quite there yet, but it was close—close enough to get a better look at her surroundings.

The space around her was nothing like the stark metal she had expected of a typical law enforcement transport vehicle. Luxurious padding lined the walls, and the bench seats were upholstered…which was why she’d thought she’d seen couches at first. The partition between the front and back of the van was solid, save for a darkened glass window. It was like some weird camper, where the driver was front and completely shut off from this strange little lunge-looking area in the back.

The scent of expensive perfume wafted through the air. Vivian turned to the source, toward the back of the van. A woman sat across from her, posture impeccable, dressed in a tailored suit that, like the van itself, seemed to clash with the policemen who had taken her down. Under the strange, soft glow that illuminated the back of the van from a single light installed in the ceiling, the woman looked at Vivian with a thin smile.

"Hello, Miss Fox," the woman said, her voice crisp and authoritative. "I apologize for the dramatics."

"Dramatics? Cops…taser…"

Apparently, she still didn't quite have full control of her tongue, either.

"Well, sure. I could have just taken you before you even entered the museum. But I was interested to see how good you were." She tilted her and shrugged before adding, "And I'd say you're pretty damn good."

"Who…who are you?" Vivian managed to ask.

"I'm Director Elise Garnett, with Interpol."

"Interpol," Vivian managed to grind out. At first, it seemed like a joke.

Why the hell would Interpol have anything to do with a pissant little museum in Charlottesville? Unless the operation was bigger than she could have imagined. Dread settled heavy in her stomach as she considered the implications. She'd been set up, and now there was an Interpol agent sitting across from her in a strangely comfortable van. Nothing about this seemed promising.

"Are you….taking me to prison?"

Garnett laughed…she actually *laughed* at the comment. "Again, no. If I wanted you in jail, you'd be in a squad car right now. Believe it or not, Interpol directors don't deal with cases of petty theft. Not that your haul tonight is pretty. Coins from the Spanish Armada, right?"

"How'd you kn—"

"All twelve of them together are valued at 2.6 million, and you were being paid eighty grand, correct?"

Vivian's mind raced. Her meticulous planning, the layers of security she had bypassed—all for nothing. But even more concerning was how this woman—this Director Elise Garnett—knew all of these details.

Garnett observed her silently, offering her comfort nor condemnation, merely waiting. It was a power play, Vivian knew, one designed to remind her who was in control. There was a game at play here, one with rules and stakes she hadn't figured out yet. But Vivian understood that survival meant learning them fast. For now, she had no choice but to watch and wait, to look for an opening in whatever web Garnett had spun.

"Are you okay now?" Garnett asked. "Do you think you can talk?"

"Yes," Vivian said now confident because her tongue didn't feel like a useless, dead slug in her mouth.

"Good Because I suppose you could still end up in jail. It really all depends on the conversation we're about to have. We have options to discuss, Miss Fox. I believe you'll find our proposal... intriguing."

Intriguing or not, Vivian knew she was cornered. And a cornered thief was a dangerous thing. But first, she needed information.

Vivian flexed her wrists, the handcuffs biting into her skin as she shifted in the plush seat of the van. Her mind raced, trying to piece together the events that led to her capture. The sting of the taser was still fresh, a violent punctuation to what should have been a flawless heist. But now, she sat across from Elise Garnett, the woman who seemed to be responsible for the capture.

Garnett produced a file, thick with documents, and placed it on the table between them. She opened it with precision, laying out photographs and reports like tarot cards predicting Vivian's future. "You've been quite busy, Miss Fox," Garnett said, her voice smooth as she scanned the dossier. "From the Louvre to the Met, your talents have served some of the most discerning clients. How you were able to lift that piece of papyrus from the Louvre two years ago…I'll go ahead and tell you right now, we still have agent studying that to see how you did it."

"No idea what you're talking about," Vivian said. But she did. It had been her riskiest heist of all. And it was the first seven-figure job she'd ever taken on. Still, it was unnerving, hearing her life's work itemized by an outsider.

"And then there's tonight," Garnett continued, locking eyes with Vivian. "I think if you'd gone a bit lower on that last attack, you may have been able to take out the officer who tased you. You would have *almost* made it past those seven policemen. As much as I hate to admit it, I'm impressed." There was a hint of respect in her tone, which only unsettled Vivian more.

"Flattery won't get me to talk," Vivian shot back, her voice edged with defiance.

"Who said anything about talking?" Garnett chuckled. She leaned forward, the light casting shadows across her face. "I'm offering you a choice."

"What kind of choice?"

"Thirty years behind bars," Garnett said, tapping the file with one manicured nail. "Or you help Interpol with a problem only someone with your skills can solve."

Confusion clouded Vivian's thoughts. Why would Interpol need her? She was a thief, not a detective, and certainly not an FBI agent, though she had flirted with that realm about a decade or so ago. Yet, there was a glimmer of opportunity in Garnett's offer, a chance to avoid the grim reality of prison life. Plus…for God's sake, it was Interpol, asking for help. Her curiosity was growing by the second.

"Help Interpol?" Vivian echoed, skepticism lacing her words. "Why would I do that?"

"Because, Miss Fox," Garnett replied, her gaze unwavering, "it's the only way you'll stay out of prison."

The air in the van felt charged, heavy with unspoken promises and looming threats. Vivian weighed her options, the risk of trust against the certainty of incarceration. She realized then that Garnett wasn't just a bureaucrat – she was a strategist playing a long game. Vivian still wanted to know how Garnett knew she'd be at that museum tonight. But she also knew those questions meant nothing right now. Currently, there are bigger things in play.

. She eyed Elise Garnett warily, searching for an angle, a way out. But the Interpol director seemed unfazed by her scrutiny, almost amused by it.

"Let me get to the point," Garnett said. "We're after a group of diamond thieves. Not your run-of-the-mill burglars. They are very good at the thieving part, but they are also cold-blooded killers. They've hit half a dozen locations across Europe. Precision jobs. No witnesses left alive." She paused, letting each word sink in. "They're escalating. And right now, they are in the United States."

Images flashed through Vivian's mind—a glittering necklace here, a bloodied floor there. It wasn't her world, but she understood the stakes.

"Interpol's been on their trail for months, but these men…they're phantoms. And we need someone who thinks like they do. Someone who can predict their next move," Garnett explained, her voice a blend of urgency and persuasion.

"Predict...?" Vivian found her voice. "You want me to think like a killer?"

"Like a thief," Garnett corrected smoothly. "You have a gift, Miss Fox. It's why you've never been caught—until today."

The implication stung. Vivian's pride flared up. She had been caught, but only because she'd been betrayed. And now, this woman wanted her to switch sides? To help the very people who were constantly trying to stop her from making a living?

"I won't do it," Vivian stated flatly. Her mind was made up. She would take her chances with the law, maintain her own code.

"Fine," Garnett said, her tone neutral. "This van is heading straight to DC. Once there, you'll be processed and sent to federal prison. You'll be processed and in a cell in less than eight hours. Your trial will be a formality."

The certainty in Garnett's voice was chilling. Vivian pictured the sterile walls of a cell, the bars closing in. A life of freedom traded for a cot and a jumpsuit. The millions of dollars she so silently sat on would mean nothing if she had no access to it.

"Or," Garnett pressed on, "when you get to DC, you board a plane to New York. Once in New York, you'll meet Michael Sterling, your partner on this case."

"Partner?" The word tasted foreign on Vivian's tongue. She had always worked alone. Trusting others was a liability.

"Michael is one of our best. Ex-military, now a tactical operative for Interpol. He has a keen mind for strategy. And besides…while I do admire your ability to go uncaught, you *will* need someone who knows the ins and outs. Someone with connections."

A partner who was military-trained. Disciplined, no doubt. The opposite of her improvisational style. It was a recipe for disaster as far as Vivian was concerned.

"Think about it, Vivian," Garnett coaxed. "Prison, or a chance to put your exceptional talents to good use. And possibly save lives."

The van swerved slightly, a reminder that they were moving toward a decision with every passing second. Vivian stared at the partition that separated them from the driver, her reflection staring back at her in the dark glass. She could see herself in that tiny cell, her skills wasting away.

"New York," she said finally, breaking the silence that had fallen between them. It wasn't agreement—not yet—but it was an acknowledgement of the crossroads she faced. Either way, Vivian knew this was far from over. "I'll go to New York."

"And you'll meet with Sterling. You see, as soon as you get in that plane, I know when it lands. We'll keep tabs on you…just in case you get the idea that it might be a smart idea to make a run for it."

"So you just need me to…what? Get information on these people and try to figure out how they think?"

"Yes. And any other valuable additions you might find along the way." Garnet frowned and reached into a sleek briefcase and pulled out a folder—thick and foreboding. With clinical detachment, she sat it beside Vivian and, apparently realizing her captive was still handcuffed, opened it for her.

The first item in the folder was a photo. The sight of it image made Vivian's stomach lurch. A woman lay on cold marble, blood pooling like a crimson halo around her head. Vivian had seen death before, had come close herself, but this... this was personal somehow. The brutality etched into the stillness of the woman's features spoke louder than any threat Garnett could have made.

"Sarah Johnson was at a bar after work," Garnett's voice was methodical, dispassionate. "From what we can gather, she was walking home and just so happened to pass the wrong street at the wrong time.. She paid with her life."

Flipping through the images, each snapshot was a punch to Vivian's gut. Sarah's lifeless eyes stared back at her, an accusation. Details of the crime scene were meticulously recorded—the angle of the entry wounds, the splintered chair leg used in the melee, the desperation clawed into the wood of the overturned table.

Sarah Johnson had not just been murdered; she'd been butchered. Garnett turned to other photos, showing more of the scene, more blood, more angles of the dead woman.

"That's enough," Vivian said flatly.

Garnett closed the folder and placed it back into her briefcase. She felt uneasy in the fact that just based on those photos, she'd made her decision. She'd help them, but not because she cared about justice—not really. No, for right now, she wanted to avoid prison. And if she was being *painfully* obvious with herself, there was one other reason…a reason she was choosing not to focus on as she sat cuffed in the back of what was presumably an Interpol van.

"Alright," she said, voice steady despite the turmoil inside. "I'm in."

Garnett nodded, her eyes never leaving Vivian's. "Smart choice."

But even as she agreed, Vivian's mind was a whirlwind of plans. She memorized every turn of the van, counted the seconds between shifts of the driver's gears, noted the slight squeak in the third wheel well. Escape wasn't just a possibility right now.

But she thought the opportunity would certain present itself later—probably when she paired up with Sterling, whoever he was. For now, she would play their game, learn their secrets.

The van rumbled on, carrying Vivian towards an uncertain future. But in her heart, she clung to the one thing she knew for sure: the instant Garnett, Sterling or any of their Interpol minions slipped, she'd be gone.

CHAPTER THREE

In her past, Vivian had canvassed some of the world's busiest museums and had been forced to travel on some of the most packed and over-crowded buses and trains. But there was just something about getting off of a plane and stepping into JFK Airport that somehow seemed worse than any of that. Always crowded, always loud, and people bustling about in a hurry to get nowhere in particular.

She was just happy she wasn't going to have to stop by luggage. As part of the deal, Elise Garnett had given her a credit card to purchase whatever she needed, as well as a cell phone that was to only be used for calls pertaining to the case. In other words, she already had everything she needed. Taking a series of deep breaths, she made her way through the airport and managed to make it outside without losing her patience.

She hailed a cab and slid into the backseat. The familiar scent of worn upholstery and faint exhaust fumes wafted in. Vivian extracted the burner phone Garnett had given her. Elise Garnett had been clear: this device was her tether to Interpol, to her chance at redemption—or so they'd have her believe. She found Sterling's number—one of the three already programmed in—and pressed Call with a sigh.

This is sure to be an awkward call, she thought.

The phone rang just a single time before it was answered.

"Sterling," came the terse greeting, clipped and precise. British, without a doubt. His voice carried the weight of authority, the kind that had never sat well with Vivian.

"Michael Sterling? It's Vivian Fox. I'm your... partner," she said, the word leaving a sour taste. "Or at least that's what Director Garnett says."

"Ah, the illustrious art thief turned amateur detective," Sterling remarked dryly. "How delightful. You're in the city?"

"Yeah Just grabbed a cab from the airport and now I need to tell the driver where to go."

"Come to 49 West 27th Street. And don't dawdle; we've already lost too much time."

She wanted to retort, to maybe make a jab at how he could at least say *please* or something. But he'd already ended the call. She gave the address tot eh driver and he instantly pulled out into the endless stream of airport traffic.

Sterling had seemed annoyed that she was here—that he'd been saddled with her. She understood it because it was an annoyance that mirrored her own. She'd always been used to working alone because her success hinged on silence and solitude. But now, ensnared by Garnett's ultimatum, solitude was out the window.

As the cityscape blurred past, Vivian's gaze flitted across the steel and glass canyons of New York, a city brimming with both splendor and sin. The sight of the city before she'd properly entered its mazes and streets seemed to whisper to her, to maybe even greet her back. She did have memories here, mostly good ones. Somewhere in the chaos of it all, there was a gallery where she'd lifted a Degas with a sleight of hand; elsewhere, a penthouse stripped of its pearls under the cover of night.

She'd sampled the city better than most, from its seedier crime-filled areas to the opulent banquets she'd infiltrated with nothing but charm and a chameleon's grace. Two months in Manhattan had given her a lover's knowledge of its twists and turns, yet even as affection swelled within her chest, the idea of staying out *anywhere* made her uneasy. In her profession, it was always smarter to stay on the move. Eight weeks in New York City had been beaten out only by a stint of three months in Paris—her two long-term stays in any place on the planet.

As the taxi slowed, reality snapped back with the abruptness of a pulled shade. The address Sterling had provided materialized before her—a building as unassuming as it was unexpected. It wasn't a museum or gallery like she'd been expecting, but an old brownstone with aspirations of becoming something new. She paid her fare with the card reader built into the back of the car, the simple exchange grounding her.

Stepping out onto the sidewalk, the brownstone loomed ahead, its facade etched with the wear of years. She could already tell it was vacant; looking into those dark, featureless windows reminded her far too much of the dead stare in Sarah Johnson's eyes in all of Garnett's crime scene photos. Pushing open the door, dust particles danced in the shafts of light coming through those windows, playing on the bare bones of a place caught between what it had been and what it would become.

The silence was absolute, a vacuum that seemed to swallow the sounds of the city whole. She moved forward cautiously, her sneakers just as quiet here as they had been the previous night in Charlottesville. She walked like this everywhere—quiet and stealthy—a habit she'd never been able to break.

Vivian's gaze tracked the length of the room, her breath catching slightly as the musty air clung to the back of her throat. The dim light cast shadows on the bare walls, but there, at the far end, she spotted a man crouched down and looking at the floor. He was quickly scribbling something into a pocket-sized notebook.

"Michael Sterling?" she asked.

Her voice startled him, nearly making him drop the notebook. She hadn't meant to spook him, but it was good to know that she could so easily sneak up on him. She stored that little nugget away for future use.

Sterling straightened, turning to face her with an eyebrow raised—a silent question hanging between them. "You must be Vivian Fox," he said, his British accent crisp and oddly out of place in the derelict New York brownstone.

"That's me," she said. She extended her hand, which he shook with a firm grip that spoke of military discipline. As they released, Vivian's eyes drifted past him to the center of the room, and her pulse quickened.

The familiarity was jarring—the scene from Sarah Johnson's files materialized before her. This was the room where the woman's life had been snuffed out.

"Seems quite ordinary, doesn't it?" Sterling remarked, following her gaze. "For a place where such a brutal murder unfolded."

"Ordinary never means safe," Vivian replied, the words edged with her own experience. It was a bit of information she'd picked up from her own jobs.

She drew the case file from her leather bag, peeling it open with careful fingers. The glossy photos within were a stark contrast to the grainy reality around her. She compared each image to the room's corners, the walls, the way the light fell languidly through the cracks in the boarded windows.

But it was the floor that demanded her attention now. There, amid the dust and debris, were marks—small but telling. They dotted the wood where the killer's knife had pierced not just flesh, but through Sarah's entire body. Each indentation was a silent testament to the violence that had been dealt out in this building. And around it, though it had been cleaned recently, the wood was clearly stained a bit darker by the sheer amount of blood that had been spilled here recently.

Vivian crouched beside the marks in the floor, studying them but not quite sure why. The brutality of it was clear to see, like a physical presence in the room that made her skin crawl.

"That’s where her body was found," Sterling said. He was tucking his little notebook into the inner pocket of his black jacket with white letters on the back reading INTERPOL.

"The report said she was stabbed eight times and hit with something solid. Maybe a bar or rod of some kind."

“Yes,” Sterling said. “Both arms broken, a fracture to the skull, and all those stab wounds.”

“Was it this brutal in the cases overseas as well?”

“Yes. Worse in some cases. There was one scene where hammers and nails were used.”

“Jesus. And Garnett said they seemed to be killed wherever a heist has taken place?”

“No, not always. Often, it was just somewhere nearby. We figure it’s been witnesses…people who were just unfortunate enough to be in the area and maybe saw something.” He frowned and nodded toward the front of the store. “The bar Sarah Johnson had been visiting the night she was killed is just five blocks down the road.”

Vivian's gaze drifted from the scarred floor to the walls, seeking a narrative in the silent brownstone. She straightened up, eyes narrowing as she turned to Sterling. "Why here? What's the connection with this building?" The air between them was thick with the must of disuse and a tinge of something darker.

Sterling paused, looking at her as if he was surprised she wasn’t already privy to this information. "It used to be a jewelry store," he said. “Real estate records claim it went out of business about eight months ago and then it was being rented out by a Kevin Bateman. Bateman was arrested two weeks ago for aggravated assault and attempted murder on a business associate.”

“And what was Bateman doing with this place?”

“Using it as a cache of sorts—money, jewels, drugs. A den for illicit treasures. Local FBI agents found heroin, cocaine, and all manner of drugs. But I'm betting they missed some of the nicer things…jewels, perhaps."

"How do you know for sure?"

He didn't answer immediately. Instead, he led her toward the back door, its paint peeling like old scabs. There, nestled in the frame, was a small emblem. Black, stark against the wooden grain. It looked almost like it had been spray painted there.

She leaned in closer, noting the emblem's sharp edges, an insignia that seemed too deliberate, too bold. "What is this?" she asked.

Sterling's voice had a bitter edge. "Their calling card. It's been found at every scene across Europe." He paused, and when he spoke again, his accent seemed to carry the weight of grim certainty. "And at the first murder here in New York, three days ago."

That emblem—a black stamp of ownership, or perhaps a challenge. Sick men taking credit for the terrible acts they'd done.

"That's bold," she murmured, stepping back. "Leaving a signature like that. They're not afraid of being caught."

"They're *very* confident. Anyway, based on the recent history of this place, the dead woman, and that insignia…yeah, I'm assuming they were here to steal jewels they knew where here. I assume they had ties with Kevin Bateman but he, of course, isn't speaking. Which is fine…the way these men work, I doubt Bateman even knows what they stole."

"You…you said the insignia was also at the site of the first victim here in New York," Vivian said. "You mean Sarah wasn't the first?"

"No. There was another. I take it Director Garnett didn't tell you."

"No, she didn't."

"Odd."

The revelation hit Vivian with the force of a physical blow. Another victim, another life snuffed out under the shadow of this black emblem. More than that, though, was the fact that Garnett had not given her the entirety of the picture. And why would that be?

Maybe she's trying to see how tough I am…maybe she's testing my resolve.

Maybe. And honestly, it was smart. Because now, thinking there had only been one murder on this side of the pond, here she was with this Interpol agent, standing in the middle of a murder scene.

"Can we go there? To the crime scene?" The words tumbled out of her before she could consider them, driven by a newfound need to solve the puzzle. She hated to admit it, but the inclusion of this emblem into the case had suddenly made it much more interesting.

"We can, but you need to be prepared. This whole thing…this case. It's not pretty, and it's not like anything you've encountered in your... previous line of work."

Vivian's jaw set, firm with resolve. She might have been a thief, but she wasn't devoid of humanity. The idea that these killers were walking the same streets, breathing the same air—it stirred something visceral in her, a craving for justice that surprised her with its intensity. And it also made her think of another part of her life, a thread of her history that she had tried so hard to ignore.

"Good," she said, her voice steady despite the chaos brewing inside her. "Let's go then. I want to see it, all of it. If I'm going to help you catch these bastards, I need to understand what they're capable of."

Sterling's lips twitched in what might have been approval. He led the way out of the desolate brownstone, his strides measured and purposeful. Vivian followed, each step taking her closer to a new, strange part of her life that she'd never seen coming.

CHAPTER FOUR

The cityscape blurred past as Michael Sterling navigated his car through the dense New York traffic. Vivian didn't think it was a rental, so assumed it was a sedan borrowed from the CIA or FBI. Honestly, she wasn't one hundred percent certain how Interpol worked when they were visiting America.

"So…want to tell me about Quantico?" Sterling asked.

Vivian was momentarily shocked. She'd not expected Sterling to know about her stint in DC when, before her time as a thief, she'd nearly finished her training to become a federal agent.

"Did Garbett send you my file?"

"She did. But only because I raised so much hell when she told me I was getting a partner on this case. She told me this partner would be unique. And looking at your file…I'd say that's accurate."

"Is that supposed to be a compliment?"

Sterling shrugged. "From training for the FBI to becoming a very elusive art thief….yeah, that's a compliment, I suppose. So…Quantico?"

Vivian shifted, feeling the weight of his scrutiny. "It was a short chapter," she replied, eyes locked on the passing scenery, the world outside tinted with the grays and blues of an overcast day. "Federal agent training wasn't quite my style."

"Too difficult?" he asked. She couldn't tell if he was being an asshole or just trying to be funny.

"Too many rules. Too much rigidity." She turned to study Sterling's profile. There was curiosity there, maybe even a bit of deep interest. "I'm accustomed to... more creative freedom."

Sterling's lips twitched, almost a smile. It was hard to tell if he found the irony amusing or if he was simply amused by her. "Creative freedom," he echoed. "Is that what we're calling international art theft these days?"

"Semantics," Vivian countered smoothly, her voice tinged with humor. "But yes, you could say I've been involved in some impressive heists. Museums, private collections – the challenge is exhilarating."

"Exhilaration at the expense of the law." Sterling's eyes flicked to her momentarily before returning to the road.

"Interpol seems to think that 'exhilaration' might just help catch a killer," Vivian pointed out, her gaze drifting back to the window.

"Perhaps," Sterling conceded, braking as the traffic ahead came to a standstill. "Yet here you are, working with me instead of serving time. Makes one wonder what changed for the notorious Vivian Fox."

"Nothing changed. I just didn't want to go to prison." She was really starting to get pissed off at the way he was questioning her.

"And if you and I crack this and nab these bastards, what then? You think Interpol will just turn a blind eye the next time you go on one of your heists?"

She rolled her eyes and level her gaze at him. "Can we just focus on getting to the crime scene?"

Sterling smiled. There was something a bit pretentious about it, as if he thought he'd won this round of what Vivian was already starting to feel was a chess match.

The remainder of the ride was made in silence, and after another eight minutes, Sterling pulled the car to the curb on the opposite side of a string of businesses: a deli, a small antiques shop, and a comics and novelty store. But it was the small park to Vivian's right that had Sterling's interest.

"There," he said. "That's where Emily Turner's body was found. I've got the case files if you want to see them."

She almost asked to see them but then decided against it. She'd seen quite enough of the grotesque in the photos from Sarah Johnson's files. "Maybe later," she said.

Sterling got out of the car, and Vivian followed. He walked a few yards up the street and then turned right into the park along a wide, nicely graveled walkway. Trees stood like silent sentinels, guarding the secrets of the grove within. Further off inside the park, Vivian could hear children laughing and playing—a slightly eerie sound, given why they were there.

As she followed Sterling to a small grove of trees to the right-hand corner of the park, Vivian felt a shiver run down her spine. She absolutely hated that she was so creeped out by the moment, by what they were doing.

As they neared the grove, she wished she *had* read the files. At least then, she'd have some idea of the importance of the scene they were about to view.

“Want to give me the bare bones details on the scene when the body was found?” Vivian asked.

"Emily Turner, age twenty-nine. A freelance photographer out for an early morning run. In my not-so-humble opinion, going out for a run in park in New York City before the sun comes up isn't the smartest thing…but I don't like to speak ill of the dead. She was discovered in this grove of trees by a man walking his dog. Her throat had been cut, and both knees had been pulverized. Both eyes were black, and her lips were both busted open. Her right hand was broken. A couple of press-on nails were missing…we think and hope it means she at least put up a fight."

She was relieved to find that he was done, not wanting to hear any other details. Through it all, they’d come to the edge of the grove of trees.

“So…you’re blaming it on her?” she said.

“Excuse me?”

“You said it wasn’t the smartest idea to go for a run at that time of day.”

“I did. But I’m not—”

“So it’s her fault, instead of the sicko who killed her?”

“I didn’t say that, Fox.” And then, as if to quickly change the subject, he pointed into the trees and said: “Right there. You can see where the body was…the depression in the pine tags. See it?”

Vivian *did* see it. “These women…are they also being sexually assaulted?”

“Not according to the coroner. It’s murder, plain and simple.”

“Am I okay to step in there?” she asked.

“Yeah. Police and the FBI are done with the scene. Help yourself. But I don’t know that you’ll find anything.”

She didn't expect much, either. But she figured that if she was here, trying to help, she should give it the old college try. This was, after all, the career paths he'd initially been interested in.

They stepped onto the ground at the edge of the grove. The grass was tall but mostly dead and wild. Fallen leaves, the occasional stick, and a good deal of pedestrian litter lay on the ground. Vivian scanned the area with a thief’s eye. She evaluated shadows, escape routes, lines of sight. Where would she run if she suddenly needed to? Where would she hide?

“So, based on this location…was the antiques store the place that got hit?” she asked.

"Yes. And rather successfully. The owner says that some unremarkable jewels were taken, but the big hit was a tiara. The poor old guy…he had it on sale for seven thousand dollars, thinking it was from the royal family, a lost item from the late 1800s. We had experts appraise it, and it's actually from the 1820s and worth *much* more than seven grand."

"For these pros to go after it, I assume it was much, *much* more."

"Seven hundred and fifty thousand."

"Huh," Vivian said.

"What?"

She continued to scan the area, not sure what she was looking for. She was on her knees, taking a closer look at the ground. "Well, how many places did these guys hit in Europe?"

"Eight."

"One body at each site?"

"Yes."

"And what sorts of things were taken?"

"Paintings, diamonds, a bracelet from Ancient Egypt…things like that."

"What was the lowest value on all of the things stolen?"

"A painting by some recent guy I'd never heard of. We're told it would fetch right around five hundred grand an auction. Why do you ask?"

"Guys that are this good—that have gone undetected for so long—would likely stick to *very* high-end items. It surprises me that they're going to these great lengths for anything under a solid million."

"Is that a rule you have?"

"No, smart-ass. I base a project on price. I have a client, they pitch me a price and if I like it, I take it. I don't care what they want stolen."

"So you don't think these guys have a boss? You think they're working for themselves?"

"Very likely. And…I think it's more than just the theft. I wonder…taking such risks for items under a million…if there might be something else to what they're doing."

"Like?"

She thought hard about it before answering. "The insignia their leaving behind…and the gruesome murders…it points to something other than theft. A criminal that just wants the goods and get the hell out of there isn't going to take the time to murder someone, position the body in a certain way, and then leave that little stamp of theirs."

"I know. I already confirmed that these assholes are bold."

"It's not just that. It's like…it's like the thefts are almost secondary to everything else. And all of the victims…all women?"

"Yeah, so far."

"So you think *every single* witness to these rimes was women? Or, for that matter, that there was a witness at each of the sites? Seems a little weird, right?"

"It does."

"Murders…all women," she said. "And then the time and effort it takes to add the murder and the stamp to the equation. If they just wanted the jewels and other valuables, none of that would be necessary…"

As she said this, her eyes fell on something…an odd color to be out here in this grove of trees, partially buried under old, brittle leaves and some pine needles.

"Do you have gloves?" she asked. "Like, latex ones?"

"No. But if you see something, you and just pick it up. Carefully, though. What do you see?"

Vivian picked up a nearby leaf, a large green one with a cupped indentation at the end. She used it as a tray of sorts to scoop up what she'd found.

"You said Emily was missing a few nails, right?"

"Yeah."

"What color?" Vivian asked.

"Light purple."

Vivian showed Sterling what she'd scooped up in the leaf: a cracked press-on fingernail, light purple in color.

"I'll be damned," Sterling said.

"And do you see what else?" Vivian asked.

Sterling came in closer, craning his neck down to get a better look. "Hairs. Two of them."

"Seems like a big clue," Vivian said. "But look at the garbage everywhere. Could just be loose hairs that just happened to fall on this nail."

"That would be *very* coincidental." He nodded and looked back to the car. "I've got evidence bags in the car. Stay here…I'll grab one for the hairs and the nail."

Sterling hurried away to do just that. While she waited, Vivian stepped back out of the grove, took a few steps to the right, and looked ahead. The jewelry shop was just barely visible through the trees. She then looked behind her, at the winding shape the path took—the path she assumed Emily Turner had been running along.

For thieves that would have been hyper-focused on their job, it seemed odd to her that they would have also somehow seen a young woman out of an ill-advised run. Something wasn't quite adding up and it made Vivian wonder if these men were thieves first and killers second or if this was all more about murder than treasure.

CHAPTER FIVE

Vivian's gaze was fixed on the sterile white walls of the FBI field office, but she continued to mull over the faces of the two dead women she was now somehow responsible for. It created an unfamiliar tug in her chest—a sense of responsibility and determination to see their killer brought to justice.

While she waited for Sterling to return from the labs in the back of the building, Vivian was immensely aware of the sensation of time dragging…of seconds literally just dropping off the clock. It was yet another aspect to all of this that she wasn't accustomed to. Vivian Fox, once the shadow in the night slipping away with treasures untold, now sat in an FBI building anchored by duty and impatience. It was maddening.

Footsteps approached from the right, breaking her out of her lull. Sterling appeared, bearing a universal peace offering: coffee. He slid into the chair opposite her, extending one of two cups toward her. His own steaming mug was held in one of his large hands as he took the seat beside her.

"Thanks," she said, taking the cup. Just from the smell, she could tell it would be bland, but strong.

Sterling nodded, his eyes scanning hers with an ever-present analytical gaze. "You doing okay?"

Vivian shrugged and tried the coffee, finding that her assumption had been absolutely correct. "This is all just…I don't know. Incredibly surreal."

"How so?"

"An art thief one moment, running from people like you…to *this.* Hinging our next move on lab geeks and centrifuges." She tried to keep her tone light, but there was an edge to her words—a sharpness borne of frustration.

"Those lab geeks know what they're doing." Sterling's voice was calm, a stark contrast to the storm brewing within her. "Are you sure it's not just being a bit uneasy in seeing how things are done behind the scenes? How do the FBI, CIA, and Interpol catch people like you?"

"That *may* have something to do with it," she said. She felt a stirring of anger but managed to keep it down. She didn't like how well he was able to hide little jabs and insults in a comment that, on its face, was meant to be funny.

She glanced away, fighting the impulse to retort. Instead, she focused on the taste of the coffee, bitter and strong, grounding her back to reality.

Sterling leaned back in his chair, the sound of his sigh mingling with the muted shuffle of agents and analysts beyond the frosted glass doors in front of them. "Trust me, working within the realms of the FBI or Interpol often involves more waiting than one might think," he said, meeting Vivian's gaze with a half-smile that didn't quite reach his eyes. "I'd love to have you think I spend all of my time busting down doors and chasing after killers. But that's just not the case."

"I don't know that I'd have the patience," Vivian said.

"Exciting jobs like yours," he continued, gesturing towards her with a tilt of his coffee cup, "come with their own brand of adrenaline rush, I suppose."

Vivian's lips twitched into a semblance of a smile, though it failed to mask here impatience. She shrugged noncommittally, her fingers tracing the rim of her cup. "Art theft isn't all glitz and glamor, Sterling. It takes patience, too. Just a completely different kind of patience."

"You know…like I said earlier, I know about your stint at Quantico. I know what you wanted to become. And I've also seen you now at two different crime scenes, so I've seen that analytical and probing eye of yours." His tone held genuine curiosity, but there was an undercurrent of something else—perhaps caution or a bid for trust. "So what happened? Why the huge career change?"

She took a slow sip of the bitter brew, letting the heat sear away the temptation to reveal too much. "Some stories are better left untold," she replied, setting down her cup with a soft clink against the table. "And I already told you…too many rules."

"You did tell me that. But that's not a real answer. I know there has to be a story there, right?"

Internally, Vivian's mind was a whirlpool of memories. She couldn't afford the luxury of divulging her past, not when every detail could be a weapon in someone else's hands—namely an Interpol agent. Yet, fragments of her paced surfaced anyway: The dimly lit lecture hall at Quantico, the weight of ambition and naivety on her shoulders, and an instructor whose piercing gaze had seen through her, who'd offered her a different path when he'd seen that she was clearly done with her current path.

Off-the-books had been his exact phrasing, a whispered promise of excitement and challenge that had lured her away from the straight and narrow. It was supposed to be a side job, a way to utilize her unique skills and pay off a favor the instructor owed. But it had spiraled into a career that now defined her. Each successful heist had etched her reputation deeper into the criminal underworld until she'd somehow become an icon to collectors and law enforcers alike.

She blinked away the recollection, refocusing on the present. Remembering her former instructor made her wonder if he'd be proud or dismayed at what she'd become. Not that it mattered; those days were behind her, and she still thought far too fondly of them.

Which made her current predicament even odder.

"Let's just say I found my niche," Vivian quipped, hoping to steer the conversation back to safer waters. She was already slightly irritated with the way he was inadvertently poking fun at her and speaking down to her; there was no sense in intentionally making it worse. Her fingers curled tighter around her coffee cup, the ceramic almost too warm against her skin. She needed to keep her mind sharp, focused on the case, not lost in the quicksand of her past.

She decided it might be smart to re-direct the conversation—to put Michael Sterling under the unwanted spotlight.

"Tell me, Sterling," she said. "If this is an Interpol case, why are we cooling our heels in an FBI office?" She kept her voice low, eyes scanning the room as if it held hidden secrets.

Sterling paused mid-sip from his coffee cup, setting it down with a clink against the tabletop. "Inter-agency cooperation," he began, his British accent lending an air of authority to the mundane answer. "Interpol doesn't have agents stationed everywhere. We work through national law enforcement bodies. In the States, the FBI is our go-to."

"Ah, so you're not omnipresent gods of justice then?" Vivian's smile was sardonic, but she leaned in, genuinely interested.

"Hardly. "We use the LEO system—Law Enforcement Online. It's a virtual private network that allows us to collaborate on international crimes." He gestured toward the bustling corridor where agents passed by, their faces etched with purpose. "Think of it as a digital bridge between police forces around the globe."

"Sounds like quite the spiderweb." Vivian imagined the threads of data crisscrossing beneath them, invisible yet potent. "And I supposed people like me would be the flies."

"Exactly," Sterling said.

They fell quiet after that, and Vivian did her best to keep her mind from returning to the days back in Quantico, when she'd had her eyes set on upholding the law. And then there had been the instructor—the man who'd almost become a lover once she'd left the academy, despite the twenty-five-year age difference. She'd pushed that asshole as far out of her mind as she could, but he did pop up here and there.

Which was one of the primary reasons she did her best to not think about those lost days.

She had no idea who long she'd been lost in her own thoughts when one of the frosted glass doors opened up and a tall, black-haired woman came walking in the direction. She glanced at her watch and thought it had maybe been forty-five minutes. Forty-five minutes of surprisingly comfortable silence between her and Sterling as they'd waited.

"Agent Sterling?" the woman asked. Her lab coat and sensible shoes told Vivian that this woman was an analyst of some kind…one of the so-called geeks she'd mentioned earlier.

"Results already?" Sterling's eyebrow quirked upward as he took the offered paper, scanning it quickly.

"Fast-tracked," the analyst said. "Like you asked."

"Thanks," Sterling said. The analyst gave a little nod and then headed back the way she'd come.

"Holy crap," Vivian said. "You got those results in just over an hour. That's…that's not normal, is it?"

"It's a bit better than average. It usually takes two or three hours—up to six, depending on the condition of the hair."

"I thought that sort of thing took days."

Sterling smiled, still looking at the paper. "Depending on the department, it can. But with Interpol involved…not so much."

This was alarming to Vivian, given her career. She truly was learning all sorts of new things about the people she was so accustomed to considering as her enemy.

"Let's see," Sterling murmured, tilting the sheet toward the light. "Marcus Belmont," he finally said, looking up at her with a glint of triumph. "Ex-security expert…a New York City local."

"Ex-security would certainly give him an edge in breaking and entering," Vivian said.

"Yeah, that's what I was thinking." Sterling looked to her with the beginnings of a smile on his face. "What do you say? Ready to go meet what looks like a decent suspect?"

She was surprised to find that she was. Of course, she wasn't ready for Sterling to know that just yet. And in the back of her mind, though she did want to find justice for these dead women, Vivian was still keenly looking for an escape route when she was ready to take it.

"Sure," she said, trying to sound uncertain. "Lead the way."

CHAPTER SIX

The afternoon sun glinted off the windshields of parked cars as Vivian and Sterling made their way through the busy streets of Kensington in the Bronx. The neighborhood's aging facades were a mosaic of history and bygone craftsmanship. The area was quaint in its own strange way, made slightly unsettling by the fact that the man responsible for the deaths of Emily and Sarah might be residing nearby.

Sterling parked alongside the curb, having to hunt for a space for a while. When they stepped out into the street, he nodded to a brownstone just a few yards away, where a narrow stoop led to a faded green door. "That's Belmont's place."

Reaching the top, of the stoop, they found the doors locked—the sort that had to be opened by being buzzed from the inside, by a resident.

"I'm not thinking Belmont is going to take kindly to visitors," Sterling said. "You're the one with a history of breaking into places. Any ideas?"

She knew the comment was just an innocent jab, but it still irritated her. "What's his apartment number?"

"3B."

She stepped forward and buzzed a random apartment. After getting no response, she tried another, then another. On the fourth buzz—this one to 5D, a gruff voice answered: "Yeah?"

"Sorry sir. I'm with Regency Floral Shop, and we have a delivery for 2C, but no one is—"

The man didn't even let her get through her fake spiel before buzzing them in. Vivian opened the door and held it for Sterling, smiling slyly.

They entered into a small but tidy lobby, taking the stairs to the right. They climbed to the third floor and approached 3B without saying anything. However, before Sterling knocked, he looked to her and said: "You should probably let me take the lead."

"By all means." She meant this. She had no intention of trying to interrogate someone.

Sterling knocked firmly on the door. Muffled by the wood between them, a man's voice leaked through, tinged with irritation at being interrupted. The cadence of his speech suggested he was wrapping up a phone-call, likely work-related given the sharpness of his tone.

It took about thirty seconds, but the door was finally answered. It swung open, revealing the silver-haired figure of Marcus Belmont. He was dressed casually but neatly, his expression shifting from annoyance to guarded curiosity. His gaze flickered between them, settling on Vivian with an unspoken question.

"Mr. Belmont?" Sterling inquired, his voice firm. "We need a moment of your time."

Belmont's eyes narrowed just a fraction, the annoyance etched on his features deepening. "I'm rather busy. Who are you?"

"I'm Agent Michael Sterling, with Interpol. This is my partner, Vivian Fox. And we do need to speak with you about an urgent matter."

"Interpol?" Belmont said, clearly confused and maybe even slightly astonished.

"Yes," Sterling said, going one step further and showing his badge.

Marcus Belmont sighed, stepping aside to grant them entry. "Fine, come in."

Vivian crossed the threshold into Belmont's apartment behind Sterling. The apartment was a blend of old and new—a flat-screen TV mounted on a wall that could use a fresh coat of paint, modern art juxtaposed against plaster that held a few dents and patches. She could almost smell the layers of history, each resident leaving their mark, now mingled with the faint scent of aftershave and microwaved food.

"Please, have a seat," Belmont offered, gesturing towards a pair of worn leather chairs that faced a coffee table stacked with technical journals and mail. "Interpol….Jesus, what's going on? What could I possibly help you with?"

As Belmont closed the door behind them, Vivian surveyed the room, taking in every detail—the position of the furniture, the books on the shelves, the absence of personal photographs. It was a space of function over sentiment.

When Sterling's voice cut through the stillness of the moment, Vivian was shocked at how blunt he was—at how quickly he arrived at his point. There was no beating around the bush with this guy.

"We're here because your hairs were found at the scene of a murder," Sterling said. "More specifically, they were found on one of the fake fingernails of the victim."

Vivian watched Belmont closely. She saw his jaw tighten, the slight widening of his eyes. Surprise flickered across his features, genuine and unguarded. It was a reaction she had learned to spot—a twitch here, a gulp there. Belmont stood frozen for a moment, his annoyance at being interrupted wiped clean by Sterling's blunt disclosure.

"Murdered?" Marcus croaked, as if the word itself was foreign to him. "You…you think I had something to do with a murder?"

"We don't quite know. But we had the hairs analyzed, and they were identified as yours. So we need to understand why your DNA was present at the crime scene."

Belmont sank onto one of the leather chairs, his posture deflated. He ran a hand through his silver hair, leaving it in disarray. "This is... *what?* I had nothing to do with any murder. Where is this scene you're referring to?"

"Cadence Park," Sterling said. "More specifically, the western edge of Cadence park where there's a tight little grove of trees bordering the edge right along the fence that separates the park from the street."

Vivian remained silent but vigilant, absorbing the space around her—the way the light danced off the polished surfaces, the faint hum of electronics in standby mode. She did her best to take in everything in the same way she would study a location she was planning to break into. The work desk in the corner was cluttered with tools of the trade—soldering irons, wire strippers, a magnifying glass. Her eyes snagged on something out of place—a lock-pick set partially hidden beneath a pile of papers. A casual oversight, or something more telling?

"Well, yeah," Belmont said. "I was at Cadence Park on Sunday."

"What time?"

"Around two. I stayed for about an hour and a half. Maybe two hours."

"What were you doing there?" Sterling asked.

"Me and a few old friends got together. Friends from college…we used to have a band up until about ten years ago. We do it every now and again, play our guitars there... just acoustic stuff, to have fun."

"Where in the park?"

Belmont's eyes were filled with fear before he answered. "Not too far away from that grove of trees you mentioned. A but further up that little trail, there's a fountain. A small one, with this weird-looking fish in the center. We set up our lawn chairs right there…that's where we play. That's where I was sitting."

"How many others were with you?"

Three."

"I'll need their names and contact information just to confirm all of this," Sterling said.

"Yeah…yeah, of course," Belmont said.

As Belmont scrolled through his phone to share his contacts with Sterling, Vivian walked over to the work desk. She saw Sterling giving her a cautionary look, as if telling her not to overstep her bounds.

She nodded, but was already getting a closer look at the tools on Belmont's desk. She was particularly interested in the wire strippers. She knew these types of tools well, and these wire strippers were used for *very* fine precision work. Beside the tools, she saw a newer model video doorbell camera. He was repairing the wiring behind it.

But the lock-pick set was the most peculiar thing. It wasn't exactly top-of-the-line, but it was a jump up from the basic kits she knew police used.

"What's wrong with this doorbell?" Vivian asked.

Both Belmont and Sterling looked over to her. Sterling looked annoyed that she was speaking, maybe not quite understanding her reason for asking the question.

"Oh, nothing. A friend of mine asked if I could optimize it so that he could hardwire it into his building rather than having to recharge the battery every two weeks."

Vivian nodded, as if that satisfied her question. In a way, it did. But she still had her suspicions.

"Mr. Belmont," Sterling said, "do you know anyone by the name of Emily Turner?"

Belmont thought about it for a moment before shaking his head. "No, I don't believe so."

"Okay. And if I asked, would you be able to account for your whereabouts every night for the past five days?"

"I think so, yeah," Marcus said. "I mean, it depends on the time of night you're asking about. But Monday, I went to see a movie with a lady friend. Tuesday I had my sister over for dinner and we FaceTimed my dad…he lives up in Maine. And then Wednesday night, I spent *far* too much time helping a friend install a brick oven at his new pizza shop." He looked back over to just desk and said, "It's the same place that doorbell is being installed."

"You used to work in security, right?" Vivian asked.

"Yeah."

"What field, specifically?"

"Security systems and infrastructure. Things like that. Mostly for small-to-medium-sized businesses."

"And you have the tools and skills to install a brick oven?" Sterling asked.

"Yeah. Frankly, it's not that hard, so long as you know where the support beams are."

"Where are your tools now?" There was a hint of challenge in Sterling's tone.

"Still there. I'm not done with the installation." He tilted his head at Sterling slightly, showing his first true signs of annoyance. "You can check with Tony. He owns the place. I already sent you his number…he's one of the guys I jam with from time to time."

Sterling looked over to Vivian and she could only shrug. Based on everything she'd heard, it sounded like Belmont checked out. Still…the lock-pick set didn't sit well with her. But she thought she'd wait to discuss it with Sterling before showing her entire hand to Belmont. She didn't want to make any missteps in this unfamiliar arena.

"Thank you, Mr. Belmont," Sterling concluded, his words polite but his stance suggesting anything but closure. He got to his feet and started walking for the door. "You've been very helpful. But please stay in the city for the next few days. We may have more questions."

"Of course," Belmont said, escorting them towards the door. "And I certainly hope you find whoever it is you're looking for."

As they left the apartment, Vivian's mind was alight with questions. Perfect alibis were rare—and those that seemed too perfect often pointed to fabrication. And then there was the location of his impromptu jam session, directly across from where Emily was found.

Too many conveniences and coincidences.

Vivian and Sterling descended the stairs back down to the lobby, their footsteps echoing off the walls of the narrow stairwell.

"Thoughts?" Sterling asked.

"Something's not right," she answered. "I mean, if his alibis all check out, we can't do much, right?"

"We *can*…but it would be difficult. Why? Wat did you see?"

"A lock-pick set."

Sterling raised an eyebrow as he started the car, the engine purring to life. "Lock-pick?"

"On his work desk. In the living room." Vivian's fingers drummed against her thigh as she recounted the sight. "And it was a *nice* set. Probably better than what the NYPD carries. He also had a set of very nice, industrial wire-cutters. The sort of tool I've used in the past. Not just the sort a home-repair guy would pick up at a hardware store."

"Could be a leftover from his old job," Sterling offered, but his skepticism was evident.

They got into the car and Vivian wasn't sure where they were headed next. "So, we check his alibis, right? And if even one is faulty, we can bring him in, right?"

"Possibly. But at the end of the day, we can't touch him without something concrete."

"Like his hair on that fingernail?"

"I guarantee you that there were at least a dozen other hair samples out there, Fox. Maybe he was just unlucky enough to have his waft across a dead woman's press-on."

"Yikes. Man, I'm starting to see how no one ever caught me after all these years…if this is how Interpol approaches things."

Sterling sighed. "Okay then. Other than checking his alibis, what would *you* do next?"

"I'd get the address for the pizza place he mentioned," Vivian suggested, her voice a mix of determination and urgency. "The one where he installed the oven. I want to see his tools for myself. If he had a lock-pick set and wire cutters of that standard just sitting haphazardly on his desk, his other tools might provide some answers…especially if you're looking for the sort of thieves that could easily break into places undetected."

"Alright," he agreed, a slight nod accompanying the word. He started the engine, the purr of the ignition promising action. "But if we're wrong about this, you'll be in charge of researching his alibis."

"Fine."

Sterling pulled out his phone and pulled up the number for Tony, given to him by Belmont less than ten minutes ago. And as he set the call to speaker mode so she could listen in, Vivian could no longer deny the stir of excitement in her heart.

The hunt was on. And for once, she was part of the hunting party rather than the one who was being hunted. It was an odd feeling, for sure, but a nice change of pace.

CHAPTER SEVEN

Vivian became aware of just how quickly the day was getting away from them as she and Sterling approached the skeletal silhouette of what would soon be a pizzeria. The windows were dark, the neon 'Open' sign unlit. Peering in through the windows, she could see fragments of plywood and unused portions of two-by-fours.

"So, Tony was unavailable to come open the place up to us," Vivian said. "What a shame. You think it was just him not wanting to deal with the hassle, or that he and his buddy Marcus Belmont may be hiding something."

"No clue," Sterling said, peering in through the window. "You think you can get us in without breaking anything?"

"Man, you underestimate me, huh? Follow me…"

They walked around the side of the building, cutting through a narrow, darkened alleyway. At the rear of the property, Vivian sized up the back delivery entrance, its padlock an invitation she couldn't resist. She rummaged through her small bag, retrieving a hairpin and tweezers.

"No actual lock-pick set?" Sterling asked.

"No. I don't say this as a joke…it's one hundred percent accurate: it's in my other bag. And your boss-lady Garnett didn't exactly give me the chance to go home and pack before this little adventure."

Vivian narrowed her focus on the lock. The hairpin slid into the keyhole, feeling for pins, while the tweezers applied gentle pressure. There was a satisfying click, and the door gave way with a hushed groan. They slipped inside, enveloped by the musty aroma of sawdust and drying paint.

Inside, the pizzeria-to-be was a jumble of construction materials and draped tarps. Vivian's eyes darted around, landing on a set of tools propped against a half-built counter. Belmont had mentioned these, but seeing them in person sparked a new wave of suspicion in Vivian's chest. There was a pretty standard toolbox—the sort that resembled a large lunch pail. She opened it up and found an assortment of tools, but nothing out of the ordinary—wrenches, screwdrivers, nuts, washers, bolts, an assortment of screws, a few anchors.

But when she was done investigating the box, she turned her attention to the large lack case propped against the wall. She was pretty sure it was the case for a drill…and a large drill, by the looks of it.

"Over here," she called to Sterling, who was scanning the perimeter with a practiced eye.

The two approached the case. Vivian opened it and found that she was right. it was not only a drill, but a very nice drill. The sort of drill she'd sued before—a drill that was not going to be found in hardware stores. She took the drill out of the case and hefted it a bit in her hand. It was of an industrial design, a high-powered model.

“Looks like a bit much for the delicate art of pizza oven installation,” Vivian said. Her fingers traced the bits that accompanied it, recognizing the type instantly. Two of them stood out; their spirals and serrated edges mirrored those she had used in the past to dismantle the stubborn locks of older European galleries.

"Bit overkill for hanging drywall, isn't it?" Sterling quipped, peering over her shoulder.

"Definitely not your average DIY equipment," Vivian agreed, her mind racing. She held one of the bits up to the scant light filtering through the draped windows, noting the minute scratches along its surface. This wasn't just any tool—it was the kind you used when you wanted to leave no trace, when you needed to bypass barriers silently and swiftly.

“What do you think?” Sterling asked.

"I think these drill bits are heavy duty…as is the drill itself." She held one of the bits up; it was the thickness of a pencil but had significant weight. The spirals around its body were tight and narrow. "This one will go through concrete like butter. It's also great for busting open the seams in iron and other metals. I've used it in the past to crack open safes. The drill…it's not quite as good as ones I've used, but its close. And even if he *is* ex-security, I don't know why someone like Marcus Belmont would have it.”

"Marcus has some explaining to do," Sterling said, his tone hardening.

"Let's just say I wouldn't be surprised if this drill had danced its way through more than just wood and brick," Vivian replied, a cold knot forming in her stomach. She placed the bit back, every detail etched into her memory. “And I think we need to go bother Belmont again. Just…a little less conversation this time.”

As they stepped through he back door again, Vivian still felt that stirring of excitement, of being on a chase. But she also couldn't shake the feeling that they were on the cusp of uncovering something far darker than petty theft—something so dark that she feared she may not be prepared for it.

***

Vivian's fingers itched for Emily Turner’s file as soon as they were back in Sterling’s car. “You mind if I have another look at Emily’s file?” she asked.

“Not at all,” Sterling said, reaching into the back of the car and retrieving the file from a sleek binder.

Vivian flipped it open, bypassing the glossy photos and notes about Emily Turner. Instead, she zeroed in on the heist notes. The text was succinct and to the point, which she liked. She didn’t like to be overwhelmed with the details. According to the report, the jewelry store across from the murder scene had been hit hard; its back door compromised, the heavy safe inside cracked open like a walnut.

“I don’t suppose you have any idea what model safe was hit in that jewelry store across from the park, do you?”

“I don’t. I know it was a heavy beast, though.”

She looked at the pictures closer, and though she wasn’t sure what make and model it was, she knew it was heavy duty. And for it to have been cracked so easily…well, not only had it been done by a pro, but by a pro with very precise tools.

“That drill back at the pizzeria…that could easily have done this.”

"But not any other drill?"

“No. This sort of safe…even a decent industrial drill but would have bent and cracked.”

“You’re certain?”

“I am. I even wonder if you’d find trace amounts of the same metal the safe was made out of encrusted into the drill bit.”

“It’s a good thought,” Sterling said. “And maybe something we’ll pursue if we really have to.”

The ride to Marcus' place was a silent one, each lost in their own thoughts. Vivian's mind worked through scenarios, angles, questions.

She was now starting to truly see and appreciate why Director Garnett had seen fit to bring a thief into the mix on this case.

They arrived at Marcus' apartment for the second time, only now with a bit more knowledge in their arsenal. This time, they were fortunate enough to arrive at the door as another resident was leaving. They entered the building easily enough and hurried back up the stairs. Vivian rapped sharply on Belmont's door.

"Marcus Belmont, open up. It's Interpol." She shivered at how odd it sounded coming out of her mouth. She also chose to ignore the brazen look that Sterling shot her way.

Belmont was quicker to answer he door this time and now his eyes looked wide and alarmed. His eyes darted between Vivian and Sterling, seeking some clue to their sudden reappearance.

"Mr. Belmont," Sterling began, his voice firm, "you're under arrest on suspicion of murder and involvement in a series of high-profile thefts."

Marcus' mouth opened, then closed. His composure slipped just enough for Vivian to catch a glimpse of something raw and fearful flickering behind his eyes.

"We just went through this!" Belmont yelled. "I'm no killer!"

"If you're not a killer," Vivian said, "maybe you know a thing or two about robberies? Breaking and entering? How to crack a safe? That's a *really* nice drill you left down at your buddy's pizzeria."

This comment seemed to register in a whole new way. He shook his head defiantly, and his lips drew tight. "I did *not* kill anyone!"

"Save it for the interrogation room," Sterling interjected as he snapped. Set of handcuffs in place around Belmont's wrists. As Sterling read him Belmont his rights, Vivian took one last look around the apartment. It was clean, organized, nothing out of place. Nothing that screamed 'killer.' Yet the evidence was mounting, piece by piece.

"Hold on a second," Vivian said to Sterling. He nodded a bit impatiently but understanding fell across his expression as she stepped into the apartment to have a look around.

She checked under the neat, angular furniture - nothing. She rifled through papers, inspected bookshelves lined with technical manuals and classic literature, all meticulously arranged. If Marcus was their killer, he didn't leave trophies or clues lying around. A final sweep of the bedroom and bathroom yielded no results. No bloodstained clothing stuffed in the laundry basket, no incriminating documents buried in the nightstand. The closet, arrayed with suits and casual attire, offered nothing, either.

"Anything?" Sterling's voice came from the doorway.

"Nothing," Vivian replied, as she rejoined them at the front door.

"Time to go," Sterling said, his tone suggesting there was no more to be done here.

Vivian cast one last glance over the room, the nagging sensation of missing something clawing at her. With a resigned sigh, she followed Sterling and their suspect out of the apartment.

Outside, Sterling guided Belmont into the back of the sedan. Before Vivian got back into the car, she met Sterling at the driver's seat. Away from Belmont's prying ears, she said: "We don't have solid proof he killed Emily," she admitted to Sterling, her voice low. "But we can connect him to the robbery, to the tools, to being in the wrong places at the wrong times. That's enough to hold him even if his alibis check out, right?"

"Yeah. Not sure for how long, though. We may have to end up running those drill bits for analysis, like you suggested."

"How are you at interrogation?" she asked.

"I've been known to crack a few folks. But I already get the feeling that there's more to Belmont than there seems. He may be a tough one."

As they finally settled into the car, Vivian cast one last glance at Marcus Belmont. Even if he was the killer, there were more of his group out there. And as that fact settled in around her, she wondered just how long she was expected to be part of a team she was already feeling mostly unprepared for.

CHAPTER EIGHT

The safe swung open and he took a moment to enjoy the sight of the valuable items inside. Tens of million so dollars in art and artifacts. But after that initial glance, he barely even cared. He looked to his partners and nodded.

"I'm going out on watch."

He saw the anger and disappointment on their faces, but he didn't care. He also knew the sorts of things they said about him after he'd cracked the safes for them and then instantly started looking for any potential witnesses. He knew they wanted him gone, but didn't have the balls to say anything. He was too good at his job. And so far, they seemed fine with putting up with his…well, his *intriguing* interests as long as he was helping them get the job done.

He walked through the cool basement and to the recessed door that looked out onto the alleyway they'd used to come into the property. He leaned against the cool metal of the doorframe, his gaze flickering between the shadows of the alleyway and the dimly lit interior of the penthouse at his back. The city's restless hum seeped into the night air—a symphony of distant car horns, muffled conversations, and an undefinable noise e' always simply thought of as the breath of a city. Paris, London, Brussels, Tokyo…they all had that underlying breathy sound to them. New York, of course, was no different. If anything, New York breathed heavier than all of them.

His position was that of a sentinel, of a guard—one leg propped within the world of the heist, the other planted in the grime of the city, ready to chase or be chased.

Inside, the muted sounds of his team comforted him. A quartet of shadowy figures as silent as the grave, working with practiced haste. He could hear the faint whirring of a drill, the soft clink of tools, and the stifled curse of concentration. They were after the vault—or, more precisely, what was in the vault.

The vault itself was a hidden behind the rows of vintage wines that lined the cellar walls. It was an unexpected nest and rather clever. A wine cellar was indeed one of the last places one might expect to find the spoils they sought—the string of pearls and a samurai sword. He could care less about the pearls, honestly. Most jewelry bored him. But the sword…well, it had been a while since they'd been tasked to take something *that* unique.

As the moments stretched on, his hands twitched by his sides, his fingers curling into fists and then relaxing. The thrill of the heist and the kill to come created a cocktail of anticipation that coursed through his veins. No witnesses had yet stumbled upon their illicit undertaking, but he remained vigilant, his piercing blue eyes scanning the streets for any witnesses...for any potential victims.

Because really, that's what it had become to him. He didn't care if there were witnesses or nor. A witness and a victim could be two completely different things. And he had long ago given up on trying to determine the difference. The murders had become just as crucial to the job as the theft. He knew the others didn't agree with it, but no one had argued fully against it just yet.

"Nightstar, get in here. We need an extra set of hands."

The whisper, sharp and urgent, sliced through the quiet tension of the night. Nightstar was, of course, not his real name. it was the codename he'd chosen when they'd been selecting monikers to go by while on the job. Just another of many precautions to ensure they were never caught.

He hated being pulled from his watch. But orders were orders. And this heist was a big one. The samurai sword was valued at a cool three million—the real deal from Japan, supposedly dating back to the 1500s.

He slipped through the doorframe, the darkness of the penthouse cellar swallowing him whole. Inside, the air was thick with the smell of old wood and anticipation. His team—four shadows clad in black—huddled around the vault's casing, their breaths shallow whispers against the silence. They'd broken into the vault already not now seemed stuck on one of the induvial cases inside. The vault was the size of a large closet and though it was filled with collectibles and rare items, they were only interested in the pearls and the sword.

"This case is a tough bastard," Lionheart muttered, his brow furrowed as he fiddled with a set of lock picks. Jasmine stood beside him, arms folded, her eyes flicking up to Nightstar as he approached.

"Let me see," he said, voice low but confident. He knelt beside the case, examining the intricate lock that held the samurai sword just out of reach. With practiced ease, he slid his own tools from his pocket. He knew he wasn't the mist skilled on his team but when it came to needing something done with a. rough yet practices hand, he was the one they called on.

His senses remained alert, even as he worked. The sounds of the city filtered through the walls—the distant honk of taxis, the muffled laughter of nightlife, the occasional siren wailing.

The lock gave way under his brute touch, a satisfying click echoing softly in the confined space. The team exhaled in unison, the tension breaking like a wave against the shore. Nightstar lifted the case lid, revealing the sword within—an ancient piece of artistry that gleamed with a deadly promise.

"Beautiful, isn't it?" Jasmine breathed, but Nightstar's mind was already elsewhere.

"Back to your post, Nightstar," Lionheart ordered, his voice slightly muddled through the ski mask he wore.

Nightstar emerged once again into the alleyway, the cold air pressing against his own ski mask. His eyes immediately caught movement—two women, their laughter piercing the stillness as they said their farewells. One turned away, her footsteps retreating deeper into the city.

But the other was walking in his direction. A street still separated them, but he saw her figure clearly. Her silhouette was a soft blur under the streetlights. She moved with the carefree grace of the oblivious, unaware of the danger that lurked mere yards away.

He leaned against the wall, a statue clothed in shadow. His heart beat a steady rhythm, finding it difficult to wait. He watched the woman closely. She was coming toward the alley but looking to the right. She'd turn there, he supposed. Maybe walk home or call for a cab or Uber.

She came to the corner, just twenty-five feet away. She hadn't seen him yet—or had she? Nightstar's instincts screamed that it didn't matter. He wasn't just here for the thrill of theft; the hunger to kill was even more powerful.

Quickly, he poked his head into the half-opened door, peering into the cellar again. "We have eyes on us." His voice was even, calm—contrasting wildly with the rampaging of his heart.

"Deal with it," Codex, the other member of their group, snapped from the vault.

The words were all Nightstar needed. A license granted, a dark desire endorsed by necessity.

He pushed himself off the wall, muscles coiling in anticipation. His post could wait. The heist could wait, *everything* could wait.

Except her. Except the kill.

Smiling, Nightstar clung the shadows as long as he could. And when he came to the mouth of the alley and looked right, there she was. She was looking at something on her phone…she probably *was* calling up a cab or some other kind of ride.

He smiled as he walked slowly toward her. "Hey!" he called out, feigning concern. "You need to get out of here, it's not safe!"

She looked up to him, a tin smile on her face…but it fell away quickly. She'd seen the ski mask, maybe even the crazy little flicker in his eyes. But by then, it was too late. His hands were already on her, and even as she drew in a breath to scream, his fist was flying toward her mouth.

Seconds later, Nightstar was pulling her back to the shadows, his heart racing with the anticipation of the violence and bloodshed to come.

CHAPTER NINE

Vivian stood at the edge of the conference table, her fingers tracing the cold metallic surface with an absent-minded focus. The FBI field office's fluorescents hummed overhead, casting stark light across a sea of documents and photos. Marcus Belmont's alibis were meticulously laid out before them; verified visits to bistros, a trip to the movies, timestamps on surveillance footage, and even receipts for a latte macchiato were all accounted for.

It was almost perfect…almost enough to clear him despite having his hairs found on Emily Turner's press-on nail. But there was a void—a gap in his timeline that yawned like an open wound.

"Two hours and seventeen minutes unaccounted for," Vivian murmured, tapping on the printout where time seemed to have evaporated into thin air. "And on the night Sarah was killed."

Sterling sat in a chair across from her, his arms crossed as he regarded the evidence with a critical eye. "He says he was at home sleeping, according to the FBI agent that ran the initial interrogation when we brought him in."

"His hairs were on her nail," Vivian said, perfectly articulating each word to drive home the impact. "How is this not enough to charge him?"

"We've been through this," Sterling said. "I challenge you to go that same spot and look as hard as you can. You'll find more air from other people. Jair that has drifted into those trees over the last few weeks or even months. You'll probably find a good deal of urine, too. If we charge him and it goes to court and these hairs are all we have to put up against these very solid alibis, it'll be a joke."

Despite repeating something they'd already discussed, Vivian thought she saw a glimmer of something that might have been respect in his gaze. They were *technically* partners, yes, but from two very different worlds. She, an art thief turned reluctant ally of the law; he, a former military man whose sense of order was unyielding.

The door swung open so suddenly it startled Vivian out of her contemplation. Elise Garnett strode into the room as if she owned the place. Vivian was so surprised to see her that it took her a moment to fully understand that the woman was indeed here, in the room with them. She was dressed in her signature black suit, tailored to perfection, her strawberry blonde hair pulled back in a tight chignon. Her ice-blue eyes swept over the room as if she could deduce the entire investigation's status with a mere glance.

"Director Garnett," Sterling greeted, standing. "Unexpected, but welcome."

"Mr. Sterling, Ms. Fox," Garnett nodded, her voice carrying confidence but a bit of weariness as well. "I'm catching a red-eye back to France shortly. I wanted to see how our little project is faring."

Vivian straightened, acutely aware of the scrutiny they were under. She felt the need to please this woman—a feeling she was not accustomed to. But she also didn't want to seem like she was kissing ass, so she let Sterling answer.

"We've pinned down Belmont's movements except for a crucial period on the night of the first murder," he said. "But all of the alibis he gave us seem to check out."

"And the hairs…that's all we have on him?"

"Yes."

Garnett nodded with a small frown on her face. Vivian was still slightly astounded that the hairs on the fingernail weren't enough to close this casé. She supposed she still had a lot to learn—and that she'd been making huge, false assumptions about how the forensics and logistics of Interpol and FBI investigations for a while now.

"And what of Ms. Fox? "Garnett asked. "How are you adapting to our methods?"

"Slowly but surely," Vivian said.

Sterling chuckled and shook his head. "She's being a bit modest. "Vivian's been instrumental. She's the one who found the hairs *and* recognized that the tools Belmont owned were far more than your standard, run-of-the-mill constriction equipment."

Had Sterling just praised her? In front of their director, no less? Vivian fought to keep her expression neutral while internally her thoughts whirred. She was still an outsider in this world of badges and protocols, yet here she was, receiving recognition from a man who represented everything she had grown to run from and distrust. It was nice to hear, of course, but she also hated that she felt almost accomplished in a way. Why the hell did she care what he thought of her?

"Excellent," Garnett said, a hint of a smile playing on her own lips. "Keep me updated. Time is of the essence."

"Will do, Director," Sterling assured her.

"Also, don't burn the candle too short… Rets up. You've got the FBI here to assist. It's been over twenty-four hours, hasn't it, Vivian?" Her tone was more of an observation than a question.

Vivian knew Garnett was right. The heavy weight of exhaustion pulled at her eyelids, and her body ached for sleep. Sterling gave a small nod, his posture, usually impeccable, now betrayed a hint of fatigue. "Rest sounds like a good plan," he conceded.

"Then it's settled. Take care of yourselves." With that, Garnett left them in the stillness of the emptied room.

"Is she always that quick and direct about things?" Vivian asked.

"God, no. That's her in a hurry. Given that she has a flight in a bit, I'm surprised she came by at all." Then, with a grin, he added: "Probably just checking up on you."

"You know, I could use a bit of sleep," Vivian said.

"Same. We can book rooms at the hotel down the street," Sterling suggested, collecting the scattered papers with mechanical precision. "Close enough to get back quickly if we need to."

"Sounds good," Vivian replied, rising from her seat, feeling the stiffness in her joints. And as they filed out of the room, Vivian allowed herself a moment of relief—a moment for the tension and confusion of the day to start sliding off. The acknowledgment from Sterling in front of Garnett meant more than she cared to admit, a sign that perhaps she had truly become more than just a means to an end to them.

Oddly enough, she wasn't sure if this was a good thing or a. bad thing.

***

The hotel lobby was quiet, save for the low murmur of late-night travelers and the soft clacking of the receptionist's keyboard. Sterling handled the booking of the rooms, and soon they were taking separate elevators up to their respective floors.

Once inside her room, Vivian leaned against the door, letting out a breath she hadn't realized she'd been holding. It was a run-of-the-mill room. Nothing special, except for the eleventh-floor view. She walked to the window, peering out at the cityscape. Eleven floors didn't allow her to see the whole scope of the city, but she saw enough—the billboards, the towering buildings, the enormous screens advertising the latest movies and concerts.

It would be so easy, she mused, to slip away from this madness, to vanish into the night like a phantom. She was a thief, after all; disappearing was second nature. She could do it right now—just head right back down to the lobby and go wherever she liked. Currently, the place she was calling home was a small, rented house in Orlando, but she hadn't stepped foot in it for almost three weeks.

But the faces of the victims flashed in her mind—unseen eyes that held an accusation she couldn't ignore. They deserved justice, and Vivian didn't think she'd ever forgive herself if she didn't at least do her best to help.

"Damn it," she whispered, her reflection in the glass like a ghost. She turned away from the temptation of escape, her focus now on finding the monsters who'd been killing these women—not just Emily and Sarah, but the women overseas as well.

She sorted through her thoughts, arranging them like the pieces of a stolen artwork she might have once appraised: methodically, critically. Each clue, each witness statement, each drop of blood—they were part of a larger whole, not too dissimilar from planning a heist.

She checked the digital clock on the bedside table. 11:10 PM. Time was slipping away like sand through fingers, and though she was eager for sleep, she also wanted a shower. Like Garnett had said, it had been twenty-four hours or more…so that meant at least thirty without a shower—and she'd been through *a lot* in the past thirty hours.

She made her way into the bathroom, stripped down, and immediately stepped into the shower.

The water drummed against her back, the heat seep into her muscles, unknotting the tension that had been accumulating there. She washed down, wanting to relish the feel of the hot water but also wanting to sleep. With a bit of hesitation, she turned off the faucet and stepped out, her skin lightly pink from the hot water. The mirror was fogged over, and she wiped it with the back of her hand, revealing a reflection that seemed more ghost than woman. The sight was a jarring reminder of the life she'd led up until now—a life that had prepared her for everything but the role of being on this side of the law.

With a sigh, she wrapped herself in the hotel towel and walked back into the room, taking note of her limited wardrobe strewn across the chair. She needed another change of clothes, something fresh. There mere idea of slipping back into those dirty clothes made her feel itchy.

Her gaze flickered to the window where the city's twinkling lights beckoned with the promise of open stores, even at this hour. For a moment, she thought about stepped out into the night, weaving through the late crowds, and acquiring what she needed. But the thought dissipated as quickly as it came, crushed by the weight of her eyelids.

"Tomorrow," she murmured, conceding to the need for rest.

Vivian crawled into bed naked, the clock casting a soft glow over the room: 11:22. She pulled the covers up to her chin, letting out a breath she didn't realize she'd been holding. The world outside faded away, and sleep claimed her with greedy, silent fingers.

Those fingers also pulled her down into the depths of dreams. She found herself back at Quantico, though not as an agent. Her instructor—the one with the hawkish eyes and a sharp tongue—was offering her a job. Not just any job, but the first real test of her skills. In the dream he came to her almost as if he was attempting to date her, dressed in a handsome suit, and speaking in casual terms rather than the more rigid dialect he'd used in the halls of the academy.

"Are you in or out?" he asked, handing her a blueprint of a safe nestled within a wall of an upscale bar. They were standing in the park where Emily Turner was killed, hiding under the grove of trees.

"In."

And lo and behold, the door to a safe appeared within the ground—directly where Emily's body had been buried.

Dream-Vivian moved with practiced ease, the combination lock giving way under her deft touch. The door swung open, and instead of the usual cache of glittering jewels and crisp bills, there was Sarah Johnson. Dead and covered ins red, sticky blood, her lifeless eyes stared up at Vivian accusingly.

Slowly, Vivian reached down to pull the body out, but the dream image was shattered like glass.

Vivian sat bolt upright in her bed, realizing that she'd bene pulled out of sleep by a knocking at the door of her hotel room.

She looked at the digital numbers on the bedside table. They glowed a harsh, accusatory red—3:12 AM. Her pulse skittered like pebbles over ice, the knock repeating, insistent. There was no gentleness in that sound, no courtesy; it was a command.

Swinging her legs out from under the covers, she pulled a sheet off with her, wrapping it around herself in lieu of pajamas. She padded across the carpet, disoriented. She reached the door and peered through the peephole. Sterling stood there, his posture rigid, his face set in grim lines that the door's distortion couldn't blur. Vivian unlatched the chain and opened the door just a bit, craning her neck and head out while leaving her sheet-covered body behind the door. When she saw his face clearly, her confusion gave way to a prickling sense of urgency.

"Another murder," Sterling said without preamble. His voice was flat, but beneath the surface ran an undercurrent of tightly controlled anger. "We need to head to the scene."

She nodded, suddenly wide awake. "Give me two minutes."

He nodded and took a step back from the door as if to respect her privacy. It was a small gesture but it meant a lot to her.

Vivian stepped back into the room, hands mechanically reaching for clothes. Her movements were quick, precise, betraying none of the fatigue that still tugged at her muscles. She threw on the same clothes, hating that she could smell a slight bit of sweat and dust from the previous day. Her jacket followed, and then she was opening the door again.

Sterling was waiting for her, a shadow framed by the flickering light of the hallway. "Are you okay?" he asked. "Do you think you're ready for this?"

She shrugged and though she knew it was going to sound cliched, the comment came out of her mouth anyway. "Only one way to find out."

And with that, she moved toward the elevators before her own answer had the chance to make her uneasy.

CHAPTER TEN

The crime scene loomed ahead, a grim stage set with flashing blue lights and the stark yellow of police tape. As Sterling pulled up behind a line of official vehicles, Vivian felt very much out of place. She was usually on the run from these sorts of lights. But now she was willingly walking into them, trying to find and stop a group of thieves and killers.

In an almost hysterical moment, as she stepped out of the car, the line to an old Talking Heads song dashed through her head. *"And you may ask yourself...how did I get here?"*

She shook her head at the question. She's lived a crazy life to this point, and it seemed like it was only going to get crazier.

She and Sterling stepped out of the car and as they approached the crime scene tape, Sterling reached out and gently took her by the sleeve. It gave her a moment to again study the scene before them. It was a tableau of urgency: the silhouettes of police officers moved briskly in the dark hours of early morning, voices crackled over radios, and the yellow tape marked the boundary between order and chaos.

"Are you going to be okay?"

"Yeah..."

"This is a fresh crime scene. I have no idea how bad it will be."

"I'll be fine," she said, even though the coiling in her guts was starting to indicate otherwise.

Sterling gave her a curt nod as they both ducked under the police tape. His face was set in its usual stoic mask, but she caught the briefest flicker of something in his eyes—a shared understanding of what lay ahead.

As soon as they were beyond the tape, a large man in a police jacket approached them. He looked to be in his fifties, his blue eyes studying them with hope. His face bore the pallor of one who had seen too much. His jacket was unzipped, allowing Vivian to see most of the pin above his left breast. Though only a few letters were visible, she filled in the rest, assuming his name was Kurtz.

"FBI?" Kurtz asked.

"Interpol, actually," Sterling said, showing his badge. "We think this murder as well as two others that occurred this week are tied to a group that has bene realizing havoc in Europe. Would you care to show us around?"

"Sure thing. Follow me."

He led them past a few other uniformed officers and down the alley to a nondescript door. It was a lower side entrance hidden in plain sight, seemingly untouched by the grime of the city. With a heavy clunk of locks turning, the door swung open, revealing a dark room that was illuminated by another separate space a bit further back.

"The owner of the building discovered the body forty minutes ago," Kurtz said. "The victim is Rachel Nguyen, twenty-six. That's about all we know for right now. And it's…it's bad…"

Stepping further into the space, Vivian realized it was a cellar of some sort—though it had been properly finished and decorated. Even being a cellar, it still spoke of an owner who had lots of money and didn't mind spending it. The air rich with the scent of aged wood and mustier notes that spoke of wealth. She knew that painting on the wfar all would fetch at least three hundred grand and the single table sitting in the center of the room would be ten grand easy.

But Kurtz led them beyond all of this, further back into the cellar. Separated from the main area by an ornate wrought iron gate, stood the wine cellar. It was impressive, rows upon rows of vintage bottles resting in their wooden cradles. But it wasn't admiration of the space of the collection of wine that grabbed her attention.

It was the body in the floor. And as she stepped closed, Vivian could smell the strong, alluring scent of spilled wine. It was an odd combination that her feeling slightly swimmy-headed.

Vivian's eyes scanned the chaos: shattered glass on the floor, the ruby spill of wine bleeding into the grooves between cobblestones. It mingled with a darker, stickier crimson that didn't belong amongst the vintage bottles.

Sterling stepped in beside her and then gently nudged past her to get a better look. Meanwhile, Vivian couldn't tear her gaze away from the body. Rachel Nguyen lay contorted, as if every bone in her body had fought against an unseen assailant. Her face was a canvas of brutality; lacerations crisscrossed her cheeks where glass shards had dug in. A piece of dark green glass from a broken wine bottle was still embedded in her forehead.

And then there were the stab wounds. There were at least five that she could see, but maybe more hidden by all of the blood: one in her neck, four in her stomach, one in her right side. Most were still leaking blood.

Vivian's stomach churned as she took in the horror. This was not just murder; it was desecration. She'd seen dead bodies before but never in this state—never this mutilated, this fresh. The world felt like it was tilting, swaying. Suddenly, Vivian found it difficult to breathe.

Air. She needed air.. With each breath she drew, the scent of blood and broken spirits seemed to saturate her senses further. She turned on her heel, almost stumbling in her haste to escape the cellar.

As she did, she noticed the black mark stamped into the doorframe on the inner side of the cellar's entrance. The same insignia she'd seen at the former jewelry store where Sarah Johnson had been tortured and killed. She took note of the sight but didn't pause to observe it. She had to get outside. She had step away for just a moment…

The alley welcomed her, and the fresh air was like water. She drank it in, taking huge gasps of it as she centered herself. She leaned against the building's side, her hands finding the rough texture of bricks almost relaxing—a reminder that this was indeed still the real world.

A deep breath did little to steady her; the cool air did nothing to cleanse the imagery seared into her mind. Vivian felt a twinge of shame for the weakness that had forced her outside while Sterling remained composed and methodical. Her thoughts drifted, unbidden, to the victims, to their interrupted stories. And as she pushed herself off the wall, determined to swallow the bile of fear and revulsion, Vivian has her first real doubts. If this was the sort of thing that was expected of her in trying to help nail this case shut, she wasn't sure if she had it in her. Canvassing crime scenes was one thing…looking for clues and digging up leads, but she wasn't prepared for this.

But she knew she had to go back in. If she didn't, Sterling would come out here to check on her. And that would be embarrassing, especially after all of the compliments he'd given her in front of Director Garnett. She did her best to draw up the nerve and confidence, taking another series of deep breaths. As she did so, she caught a snipper of conversation from a bit further down the alley, among the gathered cops closer to the crime scene tape.

"Who else had keys to the cellar?" The voice broke through the fog of her thoughts. It was crisp, authoritative—a policeman. When she turned to see who was speaking, she saw that the question was directed to a man wearing a long-sleeved tee shirt and a pair of jeans. And if the cop was asking about keys, Vivian assumed this man was the building owner.

"Only my wife and the cleaning lady," came the response, tinged with the distinct tremble of shock. "But my wife is visiting her sister in Paris."

Intrigued despite herself, Vivian straightened up. The cleaning lady. Not a likely candidate for murder but given the circumstances, she didn't think she could ignore it. Besides…in her time as a thief, she'd noy only posed in certain positions in order to get information, but had heard of her competitors going to great lengths to secure a heist. She'd once known a man who'd spent two years pretending to be a real estate developer—complete with an LLC and two employees—just to get close to artifacts from the Roman Empire.

"Excuse me," she interjected smoothly, stepping closer to the conversation. Her eyes locked onto the owner's, seeking the truth beneath the surface. "I heard you mention your cleaning lady. What hours does she work?"

The man looked confused, probably because here she was among cops and dressed as if she were just out for a few errands. "And who are you, exactly?" he asked.

"I'm here with the Interpol agent currently in your cellar. Working alongside him as a contractor of sorts."

"She's right," Office Kurtz said from the group of cops behind them. "I saw her come in with him."

"I see," the owner said. Now that she was standing directly across from him, she guessed him to be in his late sixties or so, but his white hair was combed back smooth and stylish. "Well, she comes in twice a week—Mondays and Thursdays," he answered, his gaze darting between the officers and Vivian. "Always gone by nine at night, without fail."

"Are there security cameras around the building?"

"Yes…multiple. Twelve in all, yes, we do." He frowned, looking guilty, when he said, "They're over the building, though I rarely check them unless there's an incident."

Vivian's mind raced. In her former life, cameras were obstacles, challenges to be circumvented. Now, they could actually help. There was something almost poetic about it—the hunted turning hunter, the thief relying on tools that had once threatened her livelihood. Poetic, sure. But she still wasn't sure how she felt about it.

"How easy would it be to view the footage from tonight?"

"Easy enough, but I assure you…Jenna had nothing to do with this."

"I think we should have a look anyway."

The owner looked to the cops, as if for confirmation. As he did, Sterling came out of the cellar, looking rather ashen at the sight he'd just mentally catalogued. "What's up?" he said.

"This is the owner of the building," Vivian said. "I've asked if we can see his security feeds."

"Does he think he knows who may have done it?"

It was the owner who spoke up, shaking his head. "No, I saw nothing. But your partner here seems to think my cleaning lady may have done it."

"Sir, what's your name?" Sterling asked.

"Jacob Barker."

"Mr. Barker, if Ms. Fox thinks it's worth a look, I think we should have a look."

"Very well," Barker said, looking a bit uncertain and nervous. "Follow me."

Barker led them back into the cellar but he took a sharp right almost immediately after entering the door. They entered into a thin yet well-decorated hallway and then came to an elevator. Barker pushed a button and the doors slid open.

Though Vivian did her best to remain clam, she found herself entering the elevator as quickly as she could…wanting to be as far away from the gruesome sight in the wine cellar as quickly as possible.

***

The elevator carried them to the top floor—the third, not counting the cellar—and to a small office space. There, a desk was pushed the back, housing a laptop and a desktop monitor. To get there, they passed through what looked to be a secondary sort of den, adorned with bookcases, expensive furniture, and a breathtaking view of the city.

But Vivian knew they had no time to enjoy such things. She was focused on looking at the footage Jacob Barker was currently hunting for.

"This is it," Barker said as they walked into the room. "I have an IT guy come by once a week to make sure everything is up and running.

But I know how to operate it. So let me just back up here to show you when Jenna left tonight."

As he worked his way through the night's footage, showing twelve different angles of his four-floor home, Sterling did his best to get relevant information out of him.

"Mr. Barker," Sterling said, "do you know what things were taken tonight?"

"Yes," he hissed angrily in a quick and sudden change of mood. The questioning was apparently getting to him. "A string of pearls and an authentic Japanese samurai sword."

"Have you had anyone come to you recently interested in buying either of them?"

"No. I put the sword up on an auction a few months ago but no one was willing to pay what I was asking, so I kept it." He clicked a few more times on his wireless mouse and then stepped back from the monitors. "Right here. You can see Jenna leaving the building."

Vivian watched the screens flicker as past images sprang to life, revealing corridors, entrances, and the deadened stare of the wine cellar door. Sterling also leaned forward, his eyes sharp. Time stamps skipped like stones over water, from daylight to dusk, to the heart of night.

"There, pause it," Sterling commanded suddenly.

On screen, the figure of the cleaning lady—Jenna—pressed against the timestamp of 9:06 PM, her departure coinciding with the owner's claims.

"That's her?" Vivian asked.

"Yes, that's Jenna," Barker confirmed.

Then the footage rolled on, lapsing into stillness before jolting back to life at midnight. On two occasions, Barker himself stepped into view, but by 10:55, everything in the penthouse was still and quiet.

But at 12:18, there was motion again. It was along the first floor, headed to the back of the hallway. Someone entered the front door and walked the length of the hallway. It was plain to see that it was Jenna, though she had changed her clothes. There was no hesitation, no fumbling—this was someone familiar with the area and not wanting to waste any time.

Barker stood quiet for a moment, his mouth working soundlessly. "I... I had no idea she came back."

"The front door…what would she need to get in without setting off an alarm?" Sterling asked.

“The key and the code. I change the code twice a month, but she always gets it.”

“And who else has access to the code.”

“Just her and my wife. But as I told the cops outside, my wife is currently in Paris.”

“Any idea why Jenna may have come back?” Vivian asked.

“None. There have been a few times where she left something in the past. But she has always texted or called to let me know she was coming back by.”

The tension in the room ratcheted tighter. Vivian watched the figure of Jenna Caldwell moving with a purpose down the hall until she was out of sight.

“What’s at the end of that hallway?” Vivian asked.

“A restroom and a stairwell.”

“Does that stairwell lead to the cellar?”

“Yes.”

They watched the footage creep by, waiting for Jenna to re-appear in the frame but it never happened.

"Mr. Barker, what's her full name?" Sterling asked.

“Jenna Caldwell.”

“Age?”

“Um…I’m not sure. In her thirties.”

Sterling's brow furrowed, and Vivian noticed the subtle shift in his demeanor. Something clicked, and he reached for his phone with a haste that spoke volumes. His fingers flew over the screen, pulling up the files for Sarah Johnson's case.

“What are you looking for?”

“That name…Jenna Caldwell. It sounds familiar.”

As Sterling searched, the footage on barker’s screens continue to show empty halls. According to the sped-up footage, more than an hour had passed since Jenna had showed up at 12:06. “Mr. Barker,” Vivian asked, “Are the front door and cellar exits the only way out of the penthouse?”

“Yes. Well, there’s a fire escape off of the patio on the second floor but I’ve never used it. Why?”

“Because if she came in through the front for an innocent reason—let’s say she left something behind like you said she’s one in the past—then she would likely exit the same way, right?”

“Right…”

The shock on his face told Vivian that he understood what she was getting at—that perhaps Jenna had excited through the cellar door. And if that was the case, it was incredibly suspicious, given what had happened down in the cellar sometime between 2:30 and 3:00.

"Got her," Sterling said out of nowhere.

Vivian looked to Barker's monitors, thinking Sterling has seen Jenna on one of the feeds. But no…they were all still empty as they caught up to real-time. She turned to Sterling just in time to see him holding out his phone for her.

"Jenna Caldwell, tight there in Sarah Johnson's report."

"Why?" Vivian asked.

"Because she's also listed as a former employee of the jewelry store that used to occupy he space. Employed there as a cleaning lady."

They exchanged a silent glance that communicated volumes. And with the halls still empty on the screens in front of them, the silence and the lack of new footage seemed to give them all the answers they needed.

CHAPTER ELEVEN

The city seemed to hold its breath in the pre-dawn darkness as Vivian and Sterling arrived outside a modest apartment complex—the sort that looked like rows of townhouses. The address, hastily scrawled on a scrap of paper by Jacob Barker, now led them to the door of Jenna Caldwell. The building was the sort that often went overlooked, hidden in the shadow of nicer, grander building on the neighboring blocks.

Vivian's watch showed 5:45 AM—ungodly early, but she supposed murder investigations didn't adhere to courteous hours.

Sterling took the lead, his hand wrapping firmly around the brass knocker, letting it fall heavily against the wood. The sound shattered the stillness, as ominous as a gunshot in the dark quiet. After a moment that stretched too long, Sterling knocked again, harder this time. Another twenty seconds passed before a voice sounded out from the other side of the door.

“Yes? Who the hell is out there?” a sleepy female voice asked. She sounded angry rather than scared.

“Police,” Sterling said. Vivian almost asked him why he’d lied but ten figured more people would know what *police* entailed rather than *Interpol.*

Slowly, hesitantly, the door creaked open. A middle-aged woman peered out, her hair tousled, eyes bleary with sleep. Her sharp features were softened by confusion and the vulnerability of being woken so abruptly.

“Are you Jenna Caldwell?” Sterling asked.

"Yes," she responded automatically. “You…you’re the police?”

"Interpol, actually," Sterling said, flashing his badge. "We need to ask you some questions about your work at Mr. Jacob Barker's penthouse."

“What?” she asked, clearly baffled. With despite or because of the clear confusion, Jenna opened the door wider. “What about Mr. Barker?”

“Someone was murdered in his cellar tonight,” Sterling said. “And it’s the third murder of its kind in six days.”

Murder seemingly had a way of snapping people to attention. Jenna's posture straightened, her eyes now wide awake and appalled. "Murders? I don't…why would you need to speak with me? Do you think Mr. Barker did it? Because if you do, I can tell you right now that—"

"Three murders, Jenna," Vivian interrupted, watching the woman carefully. "And we can link two of them to locations you've been employed."

"That's ridiculous," Jenna protested, her denial quick and sharp.

"Then perhaps you can explain why you returned to the penthouse after midnight?" Vivian's question hung in the air like a challenge.

Jenna's mouth opened, then closed, her initial outrage faltering. She glanced away before answering. "I thought I left my phone there," she said finally, a plausible excuse, yet something in her tone didn't sit right with Vivian. "Down in the cellar. I almost decided to leave it for the night but if I did that, I figure my boyfriend would freak out if he called and I didn't answer."

"Left your phone?" Sterling echoed, skeptical but intrigued by the woman's sudden shift from indignant to evasive.

"Yes," Jenna insisted, nodding vigorously. "In the cellar, like I said. I was cleaning it earlier, and I must have..." Her voice trailed off as if the gravity of her situation was beginning to sink in.

"Was it there?" Sterling asked.

"Yeah, it was."

"So you got it and came back home?"

Vivian took note of Jenna's reaction. It was a sliver of hesitation, a crack in her otherwise composed demeanor. Vivian had seen that look before—the realization that a lie might not hold up under scrutiny.

"May we come in, Jenna?" Sterling asked, his politeness tinged with authority.

Jenna hesitated again, her gaze flickering between the two agents standing before her. Finally, with a resigned sigh, she stepped aside and allowed them in. "I hope you'll forgive me if I don't offer to put on a pot of coffee," she said in a snarky tone.

The front door opened onto a small but quaint apartment. The kitchen and living area were connected; a bathroom and single bedroom were both located along the living room's right wall. And that was everything.

"Jenna," Vivian began, "let's talk about your work history. You've been in the cleaning business and homes for how long?"

"I don't know," she said, her tone still filled with annoyance. "Maybe fifteen years. Started with just small offices but then got into residential."

"How long have you been working for Mr. Barker?"

She thought about it for a moment before answering. "Seven months, I guess. Maybe eight."

"He says he provided you with a key and that he always keeps you updated on the code for the front door, is that right?"

"Yes."

"He must really trust you, then."

"He does."

So far, no one had sat down. Jenna was standing at the area that connected the kitchen and living room while Vivian and Sterling still stood just by the front door. Jenna studied them closely, her eyes narrowing as understanding finally sank in.

"You…you don't want to ask about Mr. Barker, do you? You think *I* had something to do with this murder?"

"Three murders," Vivian corrected.

"That *absurd!"*

"How familiar are you with Mr. Barker's cellar?"

"Very."

"Did you know about the vault?" Sterling asked.

Yes. I knew it was there, but I'd never been inside. No reason to."

"Can you tell us about the jewelry store you worked at before being employed by Mr. Barker?"

"Likins Jewelers," she said. "Owned by an older gentleman by the name of Gabe Likins."

"And how long did you work there?"

"Not long. Three or four months."

"Why so short?" Vivian asked.

The rapid-fire questions were starting to get to Jenna. She was blinking rapidly, her eyes darting back and forth between Sterling and Vivian. Vivian could see the frustration boiling up; she just couldn't tell if it was due to guilt or having bene stirred awake so early. Or maybe both.

"I don't appreciate this," she barked. "I've done nothing wrong."

Vivian stepped forward before she was aware she was going to do it. Apparently, she'd slipped into some sort of autopilot she didn't know she possessed.

“Here’s the deal, Ms. Caldwell…here’s what Agent Sterling and I are looking at. We have three murdered, mutilated women. Two of their bodies were discovered in locations you have worked at in the past year. Both of these locations were also the site of robberies—heists, if you will, where expensive items were taken. And then last but certainly not least, we have you on security cameras going into Mr. Barker’s penthouse after midnight—which he tells us is very irregular for you. What’s more…you’re never shown as going back out the front door. And that leads us to believe you left through the cellar. You know…after you got your phone.”

“So?”

“So…the dead woman in the cellar was killed sometime between two and three in the morning. So when you toss that into this already suspicious equation, there’s a lot of fingers pointing at you.”

Vivian's eyes narrowed as she studied Jenna, watching as she absorbed everything that had just been said. Her words hung in the air, an accusation wrapped in cold logic.

"Are you arresting me?" Jenna's tone was defiant, the question unexpected and almost a challenge. But Vivian could hear the undercurrent of fear.

"If you come with us now and answer some questions, it'll be peaceful," Sterling said. “Just a ride to the local FBI office and a long chat. *Or* you can refuse and make it difficult and we’ll just come back in about an hour or two with a warrant, handcuffs, and even more reason to suspect you.”

Vivian felt a small swell of pride. Between the two of them, they’d just packed. Avery heavy one-two punch. Jenna swallowed, her gaze flitting from Vivian to Sterling and back again. The defiance in her eyes waned, replaced by something that looked like resignation. Or was it calculation?

"Fine," Jenna finally said in an angry sigh. "I'll come with you. Can I at least get dressed first?"

“Absolutely,” Sterling said. “We’ll just stay right here if that’s okay.”

Vivian didn't miss the way Jenna's jaw was set tight in anger as she turned toward the bedroom, or the bit of force she put into the motion when she closed the door.

“Damn good work,” Sterling whispered as they were left alone. “You keep it up and you’ll make a fine agent yet.”

Smiling, Vivian said, “We were just starting to get along, Sterling. Why would you insult me like that?”

Both grinning, they stood in Jenna Caldwell’s living room, waiting for their second suspect to come back out.

CHAPTER TWELVE

The halls of the FBI building were as quiet and sanitized as a hospital. After escorting Jenna Caldwell to an interrogation room, there was very little activity within the lower halls. It made it that much easier for Vivian and Sterling to speak in hushed tones just a few feet away from the room where Jenna was being held.

"I think we might be on to something here," Sterling said.

"Enough to formally release Marcus Belmont?"

Sterling considered it for a moment before shrugging. "Maybe. I'd like to get more details from Caldwell before we make that decision."

"Can I ask a question that might make me sound like a rookie?"

"You are a rookie. But ask anyway."

Vivian rolled her eyes, finding that she and Sterling had somehow slipped into a comfortable comradery much faster than she would have expected. "We stayed at Barker's penthouse for *maybe* twenty minutes. And only five of that was to observe the body. Shouldn't we go back?"

Sterling shook his head. "That's a job for the FBI and local PD. The body was clearly the result of the group we're going after. For Interpol—on a case like this—it's all about getting to the root of that group. Crime scenes come and go along the way, but we have to always be on the hunt."

Vivian knew this made sense, but she didn't like the way it made her feel. She felt almost dismissive, as if these dead women didn't deserve the proper time and energy from Interpol.

"Now," Sterling went on before she could push the issue further. "I think I'd like for you to go in there and question her alone."

"What? What sense does that make?"

"Who better to crack a thief than a thief?" He smiled and added: "You seemed to really get to her back at her place. I think we work with that. Grill her the way you would another thief you were trying to serve up to the authorities. Pretend she's competition."

Damn, he does make a good point, she thought. "You understand that I've never actually interrogated anyone, right?"

"I know. Consider this getting thrown into the very deep end."

"Gee, thanks."

But the more she considered it, the more the idea appealed to her. She'd not been at Quantico long enough to study this end of things, so it would all be new to her. She *had*, however been in Jenna's shoes many times before.

I'll be watching next door through the feed. I'll come in if I think you're slipping."

Vivian nodded and then turned to the door before her confidence had time to wane. She opened it and stepped into the too-bright lights of the interrogation room. Jenna Caldwell sat at the table, her eyes tired and filled with a range of emotions. Vivian closed the door behind her with a soft click and approached the table. She took the chair opposite Jenna and simply stared at the woman for a moment, sizing her up.

"Jenna," she began, her voice silk over steel, "how did you get started as a cleaner?"

Jenna looked almost amused at first, as if she thought this was a strange opening question. "Needed the money," Jenna replied, her voice as sterile as the room itself. "It's easy work if you have the right stuff and if you do a *very* good job, people notice. I got lots of jobs through word of mouth at the beginning."

"How'd you get the job with Likins Jewelers?"

"Same way," Jenna said, stopping a moment to think it through. "In that case, I believe it was the sister of a client who was dating the son of the owner of the store…something like that."

"Any idea why the store went under?"

"Bad economy, people stopped buying luxury items," Jenna said, each word measured, her expression unreadable.

"Sounds plausible," Vivian mused aloud, noting the guarded posture, the too-careful responses. There was more here, she was sure of it. Jenna was good, but Vivian knew a liar when she saw one—even a good one. Sometimes, *especially* a good one.

Vivian leaned back slightly, her gaze steady on Jenna, who sat across the table with folded arms and a facade of indifference. "I'm curious about something," Vivian said casually, flicking an imaginary speck of dust off the metal table. "Did you know about Mr. Barker's private collection? The little treasure vault beyond the wine cellar in his penthouse?"

Jenna's mask faltered for just a moment, eyes widening ever so slightly. It was enough. A crack in the armor. Vivian filed away that slip—an involuntary response worth more than a hundred lies.

"Well, I never had much interest in his personal matters," Jenna answered, the pitch of her voice a hair higher than before. "I mean, I knew it was there because he mentioned it from time to time."

"But you never went into it?"

"No."

"Let me share something with you," Vivian continued, folding her hands in front of her. She was surprised at how comfortable this was and was really leaning into it. "I'm a very good thief. The best, some might say. It's why Interpol reached out to me, to have me help them with this very difficult case." A flicker of curiosity crossed Jenna's expression, and Vivian pressed on. "We're after a group of thieves—ones also responsible for killing women. Brutally."

She let the words hang between them, heavy with implication. Jenna's eyes were now sharp, focused, the fear momentarily replaced by something else. Vivian thought she might be panicking, trying to re-organize her rehearsed lies.

"See, I know how a thief operates," Vivian said. "The patterns, the tells, the rush. And it's an occupation where, once you get very good at it, it's quite easy to identify someone else who practices the same trade."

Jenna swallowed, her posture stiffening. She was caught in the spotlight now, the truth a tangible presence pressing down upon her.

"Thief or not," Jenna finally managed, her voice cool but lacking its earlier confidence, "you have nothing on me. This is all utterly ridiculous."

"Or maybe we're just getting started," Vivian teased. She watched Jenna closely, looking for more cracks. Jenna held her gaze, but Vivian saw it—the slightest tremor, the unspoken acknowledgment.

Vivian let the silence fester, the room's stark white walls closing in. Jenna Caldwell sat across from her, hands clasped tightly on the table. Vivian was determined not to break the silence—to let Jenna's unease do the talking. And after another twenty seconds or so, that's exactly what happened.

"Look, Ms. Fox," Jenna started, her voice steady but her eyes betraying a hint of desperation, "I clean houses. Sometimes businesses. That's what I do. I've got nothing to do with any vaults or your wild stories. I don't know how I can be blamed for simply being associated with some place where a murder occurred."

"Two places," Vivian corrected. "And not just murders…thefts."

"I'm curious," Vivian said. She opened up the file folder on the table, a collection of documents from the scenes of Sarah and Emily's murder scenes. Rachel's murder was too recent to have accumulated any printouts to go into the folder. She removed a photograph of the insignia that had been stamped or painted into the doorframe of the abandoned store that had once been Likins Jewelers.

"Recognize this?" she asked, sliding the photo across the table towards Jenna.

Jenna's gaze flickered to the image, and Vivian yet another slight break—the subtle dilation of pupils, the faint crease that formed between her brows. It was there and gone in a heartbeat, replaced by a carefully crafted mask of ignorance.

"Should I?" Jenna retorted, pushing the photo back towards Vivian with a casual flick of her wrist. "Looks like just some design on wood. Doesn't mean a thing to me."

Vivian leaned back in her chair, the electricity of excitement buzzing through her. Jenna had recognized the insignia, of that Vivian was certain. But mere recognition wasn't enough; not in a court of law, anyway. Vivian needed more.

"Ms. Caldwell," Vivian continued, her voice low and compelling, "Let me tell you what I think…as a professional thief. I think you're getting jobs at places that have highly valuable items and that you are then staking out those places and passing along information to people. I don't know if you're *part* of the group itself, but I do believe you're at *least* being paid by someone for this information. It's a neat cover, I'll give you that. And it would have worked on most people. But not me."

"Are you really accusing me of being part of a group of thieves who go around killing people?" Jenna's voice was ice, her stare defiant.

"Merely observing patterns," Vivian replied coolly. "You see, patterns don't lie, Ms. Caldwell. For a thief, a pattern may as well be a fingerprint—unique, telling. And yours are all over this case."

Before Jenna could mask her rising panic with another layer of defiance, a sharp rap at the door sliced through the standoff. Sterling's face appeared at the window, his blue eyes signaling urgency. Vivian stood up, giving one last challenging glance back at Jenna before she stepped out into the hallway.

"What is it?" she asked at once.

"Looks like we've got something," Sterling said. The barest hint of excitement layered his voice. The bureau located Jenna's phone at her apartment and cracked it. It wasn't lost at all—it was at her apartment from 9:29, when she arrived home from Jacob Barker's penthouse, until when the bureau picked it up."

"So she was lying to us."

"Yes. And that's not all," Sterling continued, handing her a printout. "These are text messages from Jenna's phone—sent to a boyfriend from the tone of it. We traced the number, and it turns out it belongs to Marcus Belmont."

"Belmont and Jenna are dating?"

"Seems like it. And even if they aren't, the connection between sort of nails *both* of them to this case."

The breakthrough sent a rush of adrenaline surging through Vivian. Jenna had slipped, and they had caught her. All that remained was to tie up the loose ends and watch as the truth unraveled before them.

"So maybe if we get them together, show them that the other is also caught…" Vivian started.

"Then they might offer up every answer we need to close this thing."

With a grin, Vivian said: "Then what are we waiting for? Let's get the lovebirds together."

CHAPTER THIRTEEN

Vivian could see the sense of unease settling over Jenna's face. When Vivian had come back into the room a minute ago, she hadn't spoken a word. She simply sat down across from Jenna with a small, thin smile on her face. Jenna Caldwell's steely demeanor. There was not a single sound within the room until the door clicked open Sterling walked in. Marcus Belmont was walking in front of Sterling, his wrists handcuffed in front of him. Belmont's sharp gaze flicked to Jenna, and the mutual expression of shock that ran across both their faces was impossible to miss.

Sterling's voice cut through the tension as he settled in beside Vivian. "Let's not waste any time," he said, his military precision morphing into something more akin to an executioner's final call. Jenna's rigid posture slackened for a fraction of a second before she masked it with practiced indifference.

"Marcus, Jenna," Vivian began, her tone disarmingly conversational, "I won't waste time on formal introductions because it's quite clear you know one another. You can try to tell me you don't, but the expressions on your faces when you saw each other told us all the truth we needed."

With no other chairs in the room (Vivian wasn't about to give Belmont hers), Belmont stood to Vivian's left, with Sterling right behind him. Belmont glanced at Jenna before quickly shifting his face into neutrality. Vivian caught the fleeting look. Fear? Complicity? It didn't matter—it was there, and it was incriminating.

"Let's talk about your relationship," Sterling said.

"Relationship?" Jenna scoffed, her voice a blade.

"Yes, relationship." With that, he placed the pages comprising their text messages on the table. Belmont had to crane his neck a bit in order to see it. When he did, he uttered a barely audible: "Shit."

Belmont suddenly looked agitated, standing with the sort of rigidity as. Aman who had to urinate very badly. Jenna chose to look at the ceiling, probably to keep most of her face occupied so that they wouldn't see her true emotions.

“So, I say again,” Sterling said. “Tell me about your relationship.”

The room was silent for so long that Vivian thought the pair was simply going to refuse to talk. But she also saw the thoughtful look on Belmont’s face. She figured he was probably trying to figure ow much trouble they might be in and if the smartest play would be to keep up the silent treatment or to play ball.

“Well,” he finally said, “it hasn’t been going on for long. Three months maybe.”

“How’d you meet?” Vivian asked.

“A mutual friend,” Belmont said.

“Who?”

But Belmont’s lips were sealed. He seemed to feel that he’d already said too much.

“Here’s the deal,” Sterling said. "Jenna, you have direct links to two of three murder-and-theft scenes related to this case. And ‘m starting to wonder if we dig into that third location if you might somehow be linked to that as well. And as for you, Marcus, an ex-security expert with access to an industrial drill and wo happens to have a rather nice lock-pic set just hanging out in your apartment? And *then* you add in the fact that you two not only know on another, but that you’re romantically involved.”

“I wouldn’t say *romantically,”* Jenna scoffed.

“I don’t really care,” Sterling said. “You add that all up, and the picture is very telling.”

Jenna's eyes darted around the room, a rabbit in a snare looking for any escape. Belmont, on the other hand, seemed a bit more relaxed now that at least a portion of their secret was in the air.

"Coincidental," Jenna managed, her voice a strained whisper. “It’s all just a big coincidence.” But Vivian could read the woman’s eyes. Jenna *knew* it sounded weak.

"Is that your final word?" Sterling asked.

"Being in the wrong place at the wrong time doesn't make me a killer," Jenna shot back, attempting to rally. But her voice lacked conviction, and her hands betrayed her, knuckles white as they gripped the table.

"Marcus, help us understand," Vivian pressed on, leaning closer. "What is your relationship with Jenna?”

"Like we said," Belmont drawled, his silver hair catching the harsh light above. "Nothing serious."

Vivian exchanged a quick, silent glance with Sterling. They both knew when someone was holding back. Belmont's nonchalance was too practiced, too deliberate. Jenna was barely keeping it together, anxiety crackling like static around her. If she gripped the table any harder, she might very well snap it in half.

"Think about what you're doing here," Sterling suddenly offered, his voice taking on a softer, more persuasive tone. "There's a very good chance you could leave this room within the next fifteen minutes and we'd never bother you again. All you'd have to do is provide us with names."

"What names?" Belmont asked, perhaps a bit too quickly.

"The others in your group. I mean…you've been caught. And from what we know, it's an overseas group, right? And based on our records, you're both American. So I think it's safe to say they won't think twice about leaving you behind to rot."

Belmont's lips twitched into a half-smile, not quite reaching his cool, detached eyes. "You're wasting your time. We aren't going to talk."

The silence that followed was heavy, filled with unspoken threats and promises. Vivian's mind raced, considering their options.

"Alright then," Vivian conceded with a nod, pushing her chair back with a scrape that echoed off the walls. She stood, feeling the weight of their stares, measuring the gravity of their silence. Time to regroup, to find another angle—there was always another angle.

As she stepped toward the door, casting one last look at the suspects, a part of her admired their loyalty, even as it frustrated her. They were protecting their own, come hell or high water. Vivian had been in that situation a few times herself. The question now was how to break that bond, to pull apart the threads of their alliance before another life was lost.

She was the first to walk out of the interrogation room, and Sterling followed a few seconds later. When he closed the door behind him, Vivian raised an eyebrow.

"Is that wise? Leaving them in there together?"

"Doesn't matter," he said. "I sort of *hope* they try to conspire. The cameras mounted on the ceilings are also audio-capable. I'd *love* to hear what they might say in private. Though, if they're smart, they'll stay quiet."

"And I do think they're smart," Vivian said.

"Please don't take this the wrong way," Sterling said, "but I expected that deal to work. I was under the impression that thieves of this caliber would sell each other out in a heartbeat if it meant their freedom."

"Some would. But two…I can't tell if it's plain old loyalty or fear that is keeping them so tight-lipped." She recalled the unreadable looks that had passed between Jenna and Belmont, the silent communication that screamed volumes. It was clear they were protecting others, but without a confession or hard evidence, they were at an impasse.

"Interpol would never let them walk, right?" Vivian turned to Sterling, seeking confirmation. "Even if they sang like canaries about the rest of their group?"

Sterling's jaw clenched, a muscle ticking as he met her gaze. "No," he admitted, the word sharp as a knife cut. "We'd have kept them, used the information to reel in the bigger fish. Whatever sentences they got would be smaller than the others, but they'd certainly see the repercussions one way or the other."

Vivian felt the sting of betrayal, however small. She had been a thief, yes, but she played by a code. In an odd way, the old adage was true: There's honor even among thieves.

"Vivian, we are not dealing with petty criminals," Sterling said, as if he'd read her thoughts. "These people are murderers. You saw Rachel Nguyen for yourself. We have to use every tool at our disposal, even if that means bluffing to get what we need."

"Bluffing," Vivian scoffed, feeling a bitter taste in her mouth. "Is that what we're calling it now?" Though deep down, she agreed…in this case, anyway.

Vivian exhaled slowly, the weight of the case still on her shoulders like a knapsack filled with bricks. She understood the urgency, the desperation. But it didn't sit well with her, the shifting moral ground beneath her feet. They needed a break in the case, and playing fast and loose with the truth had left a sour taste in her mouth.

"Let's focus on what we can prove," Vivian suggested, her mind already sifting through the facts, the evidence, looking for the next move. "We'll find another way to connect the dots."

Sterling nodded, his expression grim but resolute. "Agreed. Let's get back to it. Perhaps we should be looking into the other jewelry store…Klein's. The one across the street from where Emily Turner's body was found. We haven't connected Jenna to that location yet."

Vivian had to keep herself in check. With two very strong suspects already caught and in interrogation rooms, it felt like taking a step back to once again go diving into files and records. But then again, this was not the end of the equation she was usually on and she figured it was probably better to stay on the side of experience.

So with a final look at the closed door of the interrogation room, Vivian followed Sterling in the hopes of finding yet another clue that they could use to nail this case shut.

CHAPTER FOURTEEN

The late-morning sun cast a soft glow on the beautiful and recently renovated façade of the mansion. Beams of light filtered through the towering oaks to the left of the property, dancing on the gravel driveway where a nondescript delivery truck had just parked. Nightstar stepped out, followed closely by Lionheart and Codex. The trio, clad in matching blue uniforms and caps emblazoned with a generic floral logo, carried elaborate arrangements of flowers into the mansion.

The entire ordeal made Nightstar feel ridiculous. He felt like he was in a cartoon, a silly character trying to hide behind the overpriced, enormous bouquets.

"Ten sharp," Codex muttered from beside him. "Where the blue hell is Jasmine?"

"Probably still right pissed about Gollum getting snagged." Lionheart said.

"Well, she showed up last night even though that good-for-nothing twat was—"

"Shut it," Lionheart said. "We're close now."

They'd reached the end of the driveway, each step measured and careful. If someone discovered their ruse, it wasn't exactly the end of the world, but it would sure as hell make things a lot more interesting. Distantly, Nightstar could hear a stuffy man's voice say, "Ah, good, the flowers. At least one thing is on time!"

Good, Nightstar thought. *They're so happy we're prompt that no one is going to give us much of a look.*

As they approached the large porch, they had to start walking single file fashion. Lionheart took the lead, with Codex in the middle and Nightstar bringing up the rear. They were used to it being just the three of them; they were, after all, the core of the group. They' sometimes pick up well-researched and highly recommended freelancers depending on where they travelled. The people they'd dubbed Jasmine and Gollum had been a nice addition for the first American location but immediately after that one, Gollum had gone missing—snagged by the FBI as far as they knew.

It wasn't until after Gollum had gotten caught that they realized Gollum and Jasmine had been dating. So now that she was gone, too, it made a degree of sense but man, did it piss them off.

"Place looks like a damn museum," whispered Codex under his breath as they stepped through the spacious foyer and into the cavern-like den. Nightstar agreed, his eyes darting to the classical paintings adorning the walls, the statues that seemed to gaze down upon them with silent judgment.

"Focus," Lionheart hissed, leading the way to the den - a vast room with soaring ceilings and windows that bathed everything in natural light. It smelled of wax and old wood, a scent that somehow made Nightstar feel at ease.

The den unfolded before them like a scene from antiquity, lavish and perfect. They set about arranging the flowers, the bright petals a stark contrast to the dark undertones of their mission. As they worked, Nightstar felt the familiar prickle of unease creeping along his spine. Especially as the owner of the property came into the room to tell them specifically where everything needed to go. The old hag was on the phone most of the time, so that was fine—she didn't pay them much attention at all.

"Hey, Lionheart?" Codex said when the owner had left the room. "You think Jasmine bailed on us?"

"Maybe. I think she got spooked with her idiot boyfriend got caught. Not that I give a damn. They only got their first payment. If they don't show up again, we keep what was supposed to be theirs."

"You think we can get this done tonight without them?" Nightstar asked.

"Yeah. And as a matter of fact…"

Lionheart stopped and looked around at the hustle and bustle of the mansion. They had no real idea what the gala taking place here tonight was about, nor did they care. They were only concerned with the large office at the back of the ground floor, an office that contained a steel-hilted smallsword that had once been carried and allegedly used by George Washington.

"What?" Codex asked.

"I say to hell with tonight. I think we can probably get it done today."

"What?" Nightstar asked, equally nervous and excited. "But that wasn't the plan!"

"Keep your voice down, you moron!" Lionheart looked around one more time and, seeing that they were still alone, went on. "The doors are constantly opening and they're letting in lots of people today—caterers, decorators, florists, musicians. It would be easy to strike. But if we wait until tonight like we planned, wed have all of the gala attendees to deal with, trying to weave our way through them. I had no idea the security here would be so lacking. I think...yeah, I think we can get it done today."

"When though?" Codex asked.

"Not sure. Let's head back out to the van and get a look around."

Nightstar arranged the last of the dahlias, stepping back to survey their work. A masterpiece of deception, each bloom placed with precise intent. But as much as he wanted to feel satisfied, the absence of Jasmine and Gollum gnawed at him. It was a deviation from the plan, and deviations were how you got caught. Plus, he didn't trust them. If they *had* been caught, what if they ratted them out?

You can't think like that, he thought. *You have to focus and just mind your own business...go about things as if everything is perfectly fine.*

Nightstar straightened up, brushing a speck of dirt from his black delivery uniform. He felt exposed in the vastness of New York, a city pulsating with too many heartbeats, too many prying eyes. His home of Essex, with its familiar streets and predictable rhythms, seemed like a distant world while in the midst of a series of heists on American soil.

"Let's get going," Lionheart said. "No sense in getting caught just hanging out in here."

Nightstar's footsteps echoed softly against the polished marble as he strode through the hallway and back to the enormous foyer. The mansion, a fortress of wealth and excess, was a thief's paradise, but for Nightstar, it had become something more—a hunting ground. He adjusted the collar of his workman's uniform, a costume that felt increasingly like a second skin.

After all, if they were taking the sword today, he supposed he'd also need to plan to take a *life* today as well. And as that thought occurred to him, he understood that it was the only reason he'd been hesitant to hit tonight. He honestly didn't care when they did the job. He was more concerned about the death he'd dole out. And he hadn't been expecting to do it so soon after the last one.

But that was fine. Another thing he was beginning to understand about himself was that when it came to murder, he was always ready.

His gaze swept over the grandeur of the place, taking in the ornate carvings on the ceiling, the glint of sunlight on crystal chandeliers—details that served as distractions from the task at hand.

But then, amidst the backdrop of luxury, she appeared. Her laughter floated to him before he even saw her face, and that was all it took.

She stood by the tall windows, sunlight kissing her golden hair into a halo of warmth. She was dressed in a tight-fitting but respectable dun dress. Nightstar couldn't help but stop and stare, despite the fact that Lionheart and Codex had already made it back out onto the porch.

She was talking animatedly with the owner of the mansion—a woman whose name and face mattered little compared to the younger, gorgeous woman who had captured Nightstar's attention. He watched, transfixed, as she gestured with delicate hands, her smile reaching her eyes and making him feel both elated and nervous.

She's the one, he thought.

But more than the knowledge that she would be the body left behind in their wake, he also felt the need to know her. To possess her essence in the only way he knew how—through the finality of death. The George Washington sword, the gala, the escape plan—all of it receded into the background as this woman, this vision of perfection, consumed his thoughts.

"Come on!"

The command was hissed form just in front of him, Codex had turned around to check on him and had seen him frozen just inside the doorway, eyes locked on the woman in the sundress. Embarrassed, Nightstar hurried through the door and out onto the porch. He followed his partners to the delivery truck, each step feeling surreal, as if he were floating towards an inevitable conclusion.

"You need to get that shit under control," Codex said as they got to the van.

"He's right," Lionheart said as he opened up the back doors where a few more clutches of flowers awaited. "Besides, if we decide to get that sword today rather than tonight, I don't know that you'll have time for your….your *extreme measures."*

"Oh, there will be time," Nightstar said, smiling.

"I swear…if you get us caught, I'll kill you," Lionheart said. "I'll leave *your* bloody and lifeless body at the scene of one of our jobs."

In that moment, standing there under the clear blue sky, the world seemed to sharpen around him—colors more vivid, sounds more acute.

And there she was, imprinted on his retina, the image of her seared into his consciousness.

He leaned against the cool metal of the truck, allowing himself a moment of indulgence before gathering up another bunch of flowers. The theft, a meticulously planned event that should have been the pinnacle of their achievements, now felt trivial. That stupid sword was nothing compared to the thrill that coursed through him at the thought of claiming the blonde beauty as his next victim.

"Nightstar?" Lionheart's voice cut through his reverie, questioning, concerned. *Mad.*

"I'm good."

But he saw the fire and worry in his leader's eyes. Maybe they were right. Maybe he needed to get it under control. But as he gathered up the next round of flowers, he was already thinking of the blonde woman int eh sundress. He wondered how she'd squirm, what her eyes would look like as the life went flooding out of her.

And with that image in mind, he smiled widely behind the flowers he carried.

CHAPTER FIFTEEN

Again astounded by how quickly Interpol was getting things done, Vivian found herself scrolling through numerous text threads from Jenna Caldwell's phone. There wasn't a lot to read through, and what *was* there was mostly between her and Belmont. And Jenna had been telling the truth about at least one thing: the relationship didn't appear to have a romantic element to it. It appeared to be a mutually beneficial physical relationship. And, as Belmont had stated, it had only been going on for a few months.

Still, despite the wealth of information at her fingertips and the incredible speed in which it had been delivered to her, Vivian could not escape the feeling that they were running out of time. Based on the three murders that had all taken place here in New York City, it was becoming apparent that this group was speeding things up.

She liked to think it might be because she and Sterling had caught two of their members, creating a new sense of urgency in the group. But that, of course, could be nothing more than simple wishful thinking.

“Anything?” Sterling asked from across the table. Vivian had been so enthralled in her research that she’d nearly forgotten he was there.

"Still digging," Vivian replied, her eyes scanning the endless list of numbers, searching for patterns, for something that would break the case wide open. It was irritating to have this much information at her fingertips and not be able to find *something.*

Each tap on the screen was methodical, each swipe fueled by determination. However, she wondered if she was perhaps getting in her own way by trying to think of Jenna and her group (if she was indeed a part of the group they were after) as simply *thieves.* With the murders included, maybe they had darker ambitions. And if that was the case, perhaps trying to profile them as nothing more than thieves was a mistake. There was also the plain fact that thieves weren't cut from the same cloth; they were just as diverse and varied as people from any other profession. And the only thief Vivian had ever truly known well was herself.

Tethered to these thoughts of her past, Vivian was transported momentarily to the myriad places her former career had taken her. Faces and names flickered in her memory like ghosts, each whispering secrets of heists long past. She wasn't quite sure why her brain was trying to drudge these things up. Was she worried that this brief association with Interpol might somehow mar her future? Were her years of thievery, travel, and adventure now behind her?

Ah, we haven't really analyzed that angle to this, now have we? she chided herself.

Her brain clung to the memories, as if hugging them tight out of fear of never seeing them again. It drifted to the dusty heat of Egypt, where ancient secrets and treasures lay buried beneath the sands. There, she had worked alongside Ezra Powell, a man whose brilliance was only eclipsed by his insatiable greed. Initially an esteemed anthropology professor, he had fallen from academic grace by the pull of grander adventures that had eventually gotten him involved in several heists. Vivian could still picture him, his hands deftly navigating the relics of lost civilizations, eyes alight with a mix of scholarly fervor and criminal intent. She remembered standing in the golden hues just miles away from the Great Pyramids, watching as Powell orchestrated their final, fateful heist before the authorities closed in.

The sharp sting of betrayal lingered; it was she who tipped off the authorities, leading to his arrest. A necessary evil, she had convinced herself. But there was no denying the rush, the dance on the razor's edge between law and larceny. Well…that and the massive payday she's received when she'd been the one to turn Powell's stolen relics back to their very wealthy owner.

"Get it together already," she scolded herself.

"What's that?" Sterling said.

"Nothing. Just talking to myself."

"Nothing wrong with that. I do it all the time. It sometimes helps me to sort things out…almost like I'm bouncing ideas off of an imaginary friend."

Vivian chuckled and shook her head. "Yeah…that's not what I'm doing."

Their brief back and forth snapped her back to reality. The room seemed to close in further, the silence oppressive. She leaned back in the chair, stretching her neck, trying to shake off the cobwebs of history and focus on the urgency of the present. There had to be more, a clue they'd all missed.

"So, let's say Belmont and Jenna *are indeed* members of the group," Vivian said. "That means we have two of them…so the group would be smaller."

"Yeah…*if* they're both members," Sterling said. "But we haven't seen anything in the texts to really support that."

"Humor me. If there's a group out there stealing priceless items *and* killing people—young women exclusively from the look of it—then how would that alter the way the group works?"

Sterling considered it for a moment before shrugging. "Depends on who's pulling the strings. In my experience, groups like this are hardly ever working for themselves. Someone hired them. If they feel they have no choice but to finish the job, I feel like they'd probably crank up the speed…hurry things along. But there's also a chance that they'd abandon ship. And if that's the case, it's going to be much harder to find them.

Vivian paced the length of the records room, each step a silent drumbeat in time with her racing thoughts. Two members of the group were behind bars—Belmont and Caldwell—and yet the puzzle pieces refused to fall into place. How many accomplices were still out there? How many more members to this group. Because while Sterling seemed reluctant to come out and say Jenna and Belmont were part of the group, Vivian felt certain they were. She wasn't sure why…maybe some sort of vibe they were putting off, some sort of thief radar she's acquired over time.

A heist was one thing: the meticulous planning, the flawless execution. But murder? That tainted the game, escalated the stakes. It would take more than common thugs to pull off such operations—and it made her wonder just what sort of psycho was paying them.

"The insignia…" she said thoughtfully. "Do you think it's something their employer may have asked them to do? Sort of like claiming the scene as their own…as their work?"

"No idea. It sort of throws a monkey wrench in everything. At the start of the case overseas, we had even speculated that it means nothing…that the insignia was just included to throw us off."

"You mean like giving you a false trail to waste your time and resources?"

"Exactly."

She let out a slow breath, trying to center herself, and pivoted toward the wall-sized map of New York City plastered across the room. Her eyes traced the spiderweb of streets, so tight and interweaving that they nearly started to blur together.

"Can I guess what you're thinking?" Sterling asked.

"You can try, sure."

"You're wondering how plausible it is to get a list of stores and collectors who might be next."

"Pretty close. How plausible is it?"

"Not very."

"What if we *really* narrow it down?"

"To what?" Sterling asked.

"I don't know. The things they're stealing…it's all so random. I mean…that samurai sword is something of a curve ball."

"You ever go on a job for something like that?"

"Yes, actually," she said, having absolutely no shame about her past. "A guillotine blade from England."

"Why did the buyer want it?"

"He was obsessed with the history of beheadings. And if we want to play that same sort of game here with this group…that samurai sword might indicate that the group is interested in feudal Japan. Or maybe just swords in general."

"That *would* shrink down the list." He nodded and grabbed his phone. "That could work, actually. Sure, it could turn out to be a huge waste of time, but it's worth checking into, I suppose."

Vivian nearly laughed at the irony of it. She'd made a very good living off of stealing valuable and artifacts and now here she was, working to make sure they remained safe.

Before she had time to comment on this, Sterling's phone rang. It had been sitting on the table the entire time; when it rang and vibrated on the table, they both jumped a bit. Grinning at his own nerves, Sterling answered the call. As for Vivian, her_heart skipped a beat as she dared to hope the call might be the from the FBI or NYPD with some new break on the case—a break that would lead them to making another arrest that might bring this nightmare to an end.

"This is Sterling," he answered.

Vivian could just barely make out the voice on the other end. A man for sure, but she couldn't quite make out the words. Sterling nodded a few times and ended the call with a simple: "Understood. We're on our way."

He ended the call and took a single heartbeat to process what he'd heard. He then looked Vivian in the eyes, his focus all business and anger.

"What is it?" Vivian asked.

"Another body. And the damned insignia."

As they both got to their feet, Vivian said, "I guess that answers our question."

"Which question?"

"About how they'd respond if their group lost a few members," Vivian said. "Seems like they're ramping things up…that they want to finish what they started and get the hell out of New York before we can catch them."

This comment resulted in a shared, uneasy glance between them and ten they were both rushing out of the room, back toward the parking garage and what was starting to feel like an endless chase.

CHAPTER SIXTEEN

"Any word on what was taken?" Vivian asked as they got into the sedan once again.

"List is coming through," Sterling responded, pulling out his phone and brining up a map of the city. "But at this point, I don't even think it matters. They're moving too fast. They're getting even more unpredictable."

"This might be a good thing, though. Yeah, they're killers…but they're thieves, too. And for thieves, working quickly is essentially a death sentence. They're sure to screw up somewhere."

"Then let's haul ass to the scene and see what they left for us," Sterling said, his eyes blazing ahead as he pulled out of the bureau parking garage and into the street.

"And where is the scene?"

"A large mansion about twenty minutes away from us. From what I was told, the owner was preparing for a fundraiser this afternoon when the body was discovered."

Vivian's felt a jolt of excitement as Sterling navigated the Manhattan streets. She had many more questions on her tongue, but she left them unspoken during the drive. Another body…more things likely stolen. She tried to imagine what might happen if somehow, all of a sudden, they somehow discovered that the thieves had left the country—that they'd gone back to Europe. She supposed Sterling would carry on as usual and chase these monsters just as he'd been doing all along.

But what about her? Would she be expected to sit idly by while Sterling played out the remainder of this case by himself? She found herself oddly upset about the thought and wondered what it might mean.

The imagined scenario played itself out in her head in a few different ways and before she was aware of it, Sterling was pulling into a gated driveway. A guard of some kind stopped them at the gate but as soon as Sterling flashed in Interpol ID, he was waved through. There were two cop cars strewn in among several other vehicles. A few people were milling about on the large front porch, likely having been ushered out of the house when the cops had arrived. Vivian assumed these were people helping the owner put the event together.

Vivian and Sterling stepped out of the car. Vivian's eyes scanned the scene—police tape fluttered in the breeze, uniformed officers huddled in discussion, and a few seemingly random individuals stood in clusters, their expressions a mix of shock and concern.

"Can they seriously be considering going ahead with the gala?" Sterling's voice sliced through her observations, tinged with disbelief.

"Looks like it," Vivian replied, her gaze fixed on the stately mansion that loomed over them, its windows dark and uninviting.

"Doubtful the bureau will allow it," Sterling said. "No matter where the body was found, the entire house has to be viewed as a crime scene."

They made their way up the porch stairs, where two cops gave them challenging looks. But again, Sterling showed his ID, and they were ushered through without question or comment. As Vivian followed him inside, she caught portions of whispered conversations along the front steps and the porch—debates were underway among the event organizers, their gestures animated, weighing the gravity of tragedy against the importance of the arts center fundraiser.

Inside, the atmosphere shifted palpably—a quiet dread hung in the air, stifling any leftover chatter. As they stepped into the foyer, Vivian found herself looking down a long hallway that almost looked like something out of a small museum. A pair of FBI agents were situated at the end of the hallway, speaking with a local cop. Spotting Sterling and Vivian, one of the FBI agents came hurrying down the hall toward them. He was ruggedly handsome, his dark hair making already black eyes appear midnight black.

"Interpol?" he said.

"Yeah," Sterling said, flashing his ID for the third time in under five minutes. The laundry room door was ajar, a single strip of light revealing the grim tableau within.

"The body is this way," the agent said.

"Did anyone see anything?" Vivian asked.

"No. But then again, we haven't had the chance to speak with everyone. We've literally only been here about five minutes before you."

Vivian paid attention to every detail within the hallway as they neared the end of it. There, an elegant mudroom presented itself. The tiles were white, which made the splotches of blood stand out so much that they nearly appeared black. The other agent and the cop stepped aside to let them by.

When Vivian turned her eyes to the right, she saw a laundry room that was larger than most basic bedrooms. A washer and dryer sat against the back wall, canopied by several shelves. But all of that was nothing more than background noise compared to the body on the floor.

The woman was lying on her stomach, her arms splayed out as if she had been trying to swim. There was blood everywhere: on the floor, on the washer and dryer, splattered along the walls. She was wearing a cute sundress and because it was so form-fitting, Vivian could clearly see the two stab wounds. One was centered directly in the center of her back, just below the shoulder blades and the other lower and to the right. Her head rested grotesquely against the side of the dryer, a dent in the metal evidence of the brutal force used.

But it was the sight of the tear along the bottom of the sundress that caused an icy shiver to run down Vivian's spine. It was clearly too early to confirm, but it might be a sign of potential sexual assault, adding another layer of horror to the crime.

She looked over to Sterling, determined that she would not run away from this body like she had back at the wine cellar. And not just so she'd appear brave…because she now felt that she owed it to these women.

"You good, Fox?" Sterling asked from beside her.

"Yeah. I'm fine."

Sterling nodded, his eyes sweeping over the scene slowly, as if committing every single detail to memory. Without taking his eyes away from the body, Sterling tilted his head in the direction of the agent. "Who owns the house?" he asked.

"Amanda and Charles Hankins."

"Where are they?"

"Well, Charles is in Japan on business. But Amanda Hankins is in the den with another pair of cops."

"Thanks."

When Sterling left the room, Vivian followed. She was once again confused about how easily and almost casually Sterling was able to leave the body behind. Yes, he'd already explained to her that getting a story from the body was the job of the feds, but still…it felt wrong. She said nothing, though, as they made their way through the enormous halls and spaces of the Hankins home.

They found Amelia Hankins in the den just as the agent had said. It was an enormous room, lined with huge paintings elegant bookshelves, and held the ghosts of celebrations past. She was sitting in an armchair, her fingers clutching a delicate teacup. The china was clinking against the saucer like distant church bells. Vivian took note of the way Amelia's eyes flitted between them and the hallway leading to the laundry room.

The cops who were standing to both sides of her took notice of Sterling and Vivian. They both seemed relieved at the presence of someone else in the room, taking steps back to non-verbally let Sterling and Vivian know the floor was now theirs.

"Mrs. Hankins," Sterling began, his voice gentle yet firm, "I'm sorry for this intrusion, especially under such circumstances."

The woman lifted her chin, a semblance of composure settling over her features. Vivian guessed her to be in her mid-to-late fifties. "But you need to ask questions…yes, I understand. Go on."

Her voice was low and trembling; Vivian was pretty sure the woman was just trying to put on a front—the sort of woman who wanted no one to know she was shaken.

"The victim…did you know her personally?"

She nodded and said, "Laura Ramirez. I hate to say I'm not exactly sure what she did…her job, I mean. Something with the city and marketing, I believe. She was going to be part of the arts center this fundraiser was supposed to be raising money for.

"Was this the first time she'd ever been to your home?" Vivian asked.

Mrs. Hankins thought about it for a moment before answering. "Yes, I believe so."

"How often did you speak to her?" Sterling asked.

"Not very often. Maybe once or twice a month, and always about the arts…theaters and musicals, galleries…things like that."

"And when was the last time you saw her alive?"

"Less than ten minutes before someone found her body."

"Who *did* find it?" Vivian asked.

"One of the caterers. They went back there to get a set of new tablecloths out of the dryer and found her like that."

The killers might still be here, Vivian thought. *That's a quick turnaround.*

"Mrs. Hankins," Sterling interjected, "have you ever hired a cleaner named Jenna Caldwell?"

Amelia blinked, the question dragging her back from the brink of sorrow. The question seemed to shock her a bit as it was clearly one of the last things she'd expected to be asked about in the wake of Laura's murder.

"Yes, I have. Jenna came highly recommended. She cleaned the house three days ago, in fact…to prepare for tonight." Her eyes sharpened, a sudden understanding dawning. "Is she involved in this somehow?"

Vivian exchanged a glance with Sterling. Another piece added to their suspect puzzle. Jenna Caldwell was now linked to yet another murder scene. Vivian's mind raced. They were close to something, she could feel it.

"Mrs. Hankins," Vivian said. Can you tell us who has been in the house today other than Ms. Ramirez, the cops, and the FBI?"

The older woman's hands fluttered like captive birds as she recounted the day's visitors. "The caterer came early to prepare, then the florists arrived with their arrangements. And two people from NYU—they're very interested in our art program." Her voice trailed off, eyes darting to a side door where murmurs drifted from within.

"Did you interact with any of these individuals?" Sterling asked.

"Only briefly with the caterers," Amelia replied. "But I spoke at length with the representatives from NYU. They left long before Laura was…was killed, though. Oh, and the caterer is still here, finalizing things for the event. I believe the FBI agents were speaking with him."

"Do you know where?" Sterling asked. "I'd like to speak with them."

Vivian was thinking the same thing. The caterer had discovered the body, according to Mrs. Hankins. Caterers would have an easy explanation for bringing a knife inside the house.

"Check the kitchen. It's across the other side of the foyer and to the left."

"Thank you," Sterling said. He gave Vivian a nod, and they moved toward the kitchen, leaving Amelia to her troubled solitude.

The kitchen was surprisingly minimal. The surfaces were cleaned to perfection but the space itself didn't boast of the elegance and money that the rest of the house did. Currently, he was in the kitchen by himself—a man of medium height, with a dusting of flour on his apron and an earnest expression that seemed out of place amid what had recently happened in the house. As they approached, he looked up from his work, his face creasing with concern.

“More cops?” he asked.

“Interpol,” Sterling said. “You’re the caterer, right?”

“I am. Dennis Costello.”

“I’m Agent Sterling, and this is my consultant, Agent Fox.”

Vivian nearly laughed out loud at the introduction but managed to keep her cool.

“And *Interpol* is looking into this murder?” Costello asked.

“Yes. It’s linked to a few other murders. Which makes this a very important conversation. Now…*you* discovered the body, is that correct?”

“I did.” There was a rasp in his voice, as if the wind had been taken out of him as he recalled the moment.

“But you’re still here?” Vivian asked.

“Yes. The cops okayed it…though, I don’t see how than Hankins woman expects to still have the event after what happened.”

“When you saw the body,” Sterling said, “had you seen anything out of place or just *strange* leading up to that moment?”

He paused, considering the question. "Well, everything seemed normal enough, I suppose. Orderly and neat. I mean, I suppose the florists caught my attention for a moment. They were a bit odd."

"Odd? How so?" Sterling asked.

"They were very quiet, kept to themselves. Their uniforms were crisp, professional," the caterer explained. "But their van—it was plain, without a logo. Looked rented, maybe." He shrugged in a lazy manner. "Could be nothing. Probably *is* nothing. It just didn't sit right with me."

"Did you see them leave?" Vivian pressed.

"No," he shook his head. "I've been in here since early morning, only stepping out briefly to take calls. I only saw them because I was coming back inside from one of those calls."

“Any idea how many florists were here?” Vivian asked.

“I saw three. But I guess there could have been more in the van.”

Sterling exchanged a look with Vivian, a silent conversation passing between them. “And how about the victim, Lauren. Did you know her?”

“No. Just met her for the first time today. Seemed like a sweet girl. I just…Christ, I don’t even know why I’m still here. Seems like madness.”

“I think it’s perfectly fine if you saw fit to leave,” Vivian said.

“I think I will after I finish this cake. Someone else can handle the icing. And if they end up not having the event…well, then, Mrs.

Hankins can have herself some *very* expensive cake." He sighed deeply and gave them both a shaky glance. "Anything else?"

"No, that will be all," Sterling said. "Thanks for your time." Sterling offered a curt nod as they left the caterer to his duties, his innocence apparent even to the most skeptical eye.

As they walked away, the pieces of the puzzle in Vivian's mind began shifting, clicking into place with each step. Uniforms without logos, a nondescript van—these details painted a picture of careful planning and impersonal execution. The killer was meticulous, hiding in plain sight. And they apparently knew how to get in just about anywhere. *And* they'd done their planning. To be posing as florists, they'd *known* the Hankins residence would be prime for hitting today as they prepared for the fundraiser.

"Let's get back to Amelia again," Vivian murmured, her gaze steely. "We need to see if she remembers anything else about those florists."

Sterling nodded, his stride matching hers as they retraced their steps through the labyrinthine halls of the mansion. They found her sitting in the same armchair, the cops still book-ending her. She was speaking to someone on her cellphone but when she saw Vivian and Sterling re-enter the room, she quickly wrapped the call up in order to give them her full attention.

"Sorry, Mrs. Hankins," Sterling said. "It looks like we're going to have to bother you one more time."

"That's perfectly fine," she said. "That call was with one of the VPs at NYU. Seems this little event won't be taking place tonight, anyway. What can I do for you?"

Vivian didn't exactly think the woman was *trying* to be cold and uncaring, but that's exactly how she was coming off. Because she tended to have a loose and honest tongue when it came to rude people, Vivian decided to remain quiet and let Sterling do all of the talking.

"Your caterer mentioned coming across some florists that were here earlier," he said. "Do you recall seeing them?"

"Yes. They set up all the flowers that are currently in the other den space."

"And did you speak with them?"

"No. In fact, they were very quiet and methodical. They kept to themselves, did their job, and then, as far as I know, they left."

"Did you see the van they came in?"

She shook her head and said, "No."

“Do you happen to have security camera set up on the property?” Sterling asked.

"Yes, yes, of course. Six of them, actually. Three are I the back yard because it’s just such a big space.”

“I assume you have one that looks out over the front yard and the driveway as well?”

“I do. Actually, hold on…"

She fumbled with her phone, swiping through screens with trembling fingers. Vivian watched, hyperaware of every motion, every flicker of emotion across the woman's face as she pulled up an app that accessed each of the cameras.

"Here," Amelia finally said, holding out the device towards them. The screen showed surprisingly clear footage of the outside of the house. “You can backtrack easily enough,” she explained. “Just pick the angle and then scroll back. It does have a limit of twelve hours, though. Any more than that, and it’s considered archival and we have to sing into the account on a computer.”

“That’s fine,” Sterling said. “I have no intentions of going back that far.”

Vivian watched over his shoulder as he navigated the app. It was designed quite simply, and within just five seconds, he was backtracking the footage from the camera installed out front. It was angled from the center of the porch, facing down onto the driveway and the yard. He did not have to search for long. Footage filmed from just thirty-nine minutes ago showed a van backing up into the frame—though, because he was playing the footage in reverse, it was actually the van *leaving*.

He backtracked a bit farther and didn’t stop until all three people mentioned by the caterer were standing around the van. As for the van itself, it was black and nondescript but for its lack of identifying marks.

"Can you zoom in on the license plate?" Vivian asked, her voice calm but insistent.

“Just pinch and pull, like a photo,” Amelia said from behind them.

"Got it," Sterling announced. He snapped a screenshot and then messaged it to himself. He then went back to the footage, still zoomed in. Vivian watched, trying to get a glance at least once of the faces. Two were visible in profile. All she could tell for certain was that at least two of them were men, and one had a buzz-cut hairstyle.

“We can check over all of this in a second,” Sullivan said. “For now, we need to get an all-points bulletin on this van.”

He instantly called up someone. Vivian assumed it was one of the bureau contacts but honestly had no idea. It was one of the areas within this little gig that made her feel as if she still wasn't fully part of the show. But as he read the license plate number out to whoever was on the other end, she felt that they might finally be coming to the tail end of this thing.

But deep down, she reminded herself that she knew how thieves worked. While the lead on this van and the odd florists did indeed seem to be huge, she also found it hard to believe that such skilled and practiced thieves would slip up in such a way.

Maybe this was a trick of some kind, and while she and Sterling were ensnared in it, maybe the thieves and killers were making their next moves.

CHAPTER SEVENTEEN

Vivian stood still as the bustling crime scene at Amelia Hankins' house swirled around her. She focused on the grainy image of the van captured by a security camera, a key piece in the puzzle that had just clicked into place. The APB had gone out with urgency, and it wasn't long before they had a name to go with the plates: Liam Wright.

"Looks like he's some sort of freelance delivery driver, based on the bureau database," Sterling said, reading from his phone, his voice cutting through the clamor of the house.

"Seems convenient," Vivian said. This scant information gave sparse details on Liam Wright's profile, but his occupation spoke volumes to her. He was mobile, always on the move. A perfect cover for a thief—or a killer.

With no immediate way to track him, they were left to play the waiting game. Vivian hated waiting; it felt like surrender. She cast a glance at Sterling, who seemed equally ill at ease with the forced pause in their pursuit. Instead, he'd turned his attention to the security footage again, looking for clear shots of the thieves faces or any discerning features such as tattoos.

"Any thief worth their salt is going to have a tattoo covered up," Vivian said.

"I know. But these bastards…they're good. On the way into the house, their faces are covered with the flowers they're bringing in. And on the way out, they keep their heads low. And this bag…"

Sterling pointed to a long duffle bag one of the so-called florists was carrying. It's lumpy and pretty much disheveled when they go inside the second time, hanging over this guy's shoulder. But when they come out…"

"It's not full," Vivian said, squinting at the phone screen," but there's definitely something in it."

"Looks that way."

"Mrs. Hankins," Vivian called, her tone shifting to one of gentle authority, "may we have a look around? See if anything was stolen?"

Amelia Hankins, a portrait of composure despite the chaos, nodded. "Of course. Whatever helps." She sounded a bit off-kilter—whether from the murder in her home or the fact that the fundraiser was going to be cancelled was anyone's guess.

"Can you show us around? Maybe take us by where any high-value items are placed and let us know if anything is missing?"

"Very well."

Vivian and Sterling followed Amelia Hankins through the house, moving past uniformed officers and the white noise of forensic analysis. They bypassed the hallway that dead-ended at the mudroom. As they walked by it, Vivian looked down the hall in the direction of the mudroom. Cops and FBI agents were filtering in and out, the body of Laura Ramirez drawing them in.

Beyond the kitchen, in the secondary den where the florists had set up their bouquets, they came to a staircase that led both up and down. Amelia led them down the stairs, her footsteps measured and careful.

"The only true high-value items in this house are in my husband's study," she said. "Why he insisted on having his study downstairs is beyond me. damned room feels like a cavern."

When they arrived there, though, Vivian found nothing cavern-like about it. It was a room steeped in history, lined with bookshelves and the scent of aged leather. It was borderline pretentious, the sort of study a rich man that cared about appearances might have. She was willing to bet over three quarters of the books on the shelves had never even been opened.

"Please, Mrs. Hankins," Sterling said. "Have a look around and let us know if you see anything missing or out of place."

As Amelia Hankins did as she was asked, Vivian's eyes scanned the room methodically. It was a treasure trove for any collector: first editions, antique globes, and artifacts that whispered stories of the past. As she moved through the study, her senses sharpened, each item demanding consideration.

"Let's start with what we can see," Sterling suggested pragmatically, his gaze following hers. "Any empty spaces on these shelves?"

Amelia's eyes clouded with thought as she surveyed the room, then slowly began to approach a built-in bookshelf. The shelves were quite deep and as the woman neared it, Vivian could already see the space that had captured her attention.

Amelia's fingers trembled as they traced the outline of the empty space. There was a thin, almost transparent mount of some kind sitting on the shelf. And it was empty.

"Here," she said. "Right here…"

"What should be there?" Vivian asked.

"A blade…a sword of some kind. A short sword…I think that's what it was called. It once belonged to George Washington."

"You're certain?" Sterling asked.

"Yes. Positive. It always sat here. He *really* treasured it. I think he spent upwards of ninety thousand dollars on that thing."

Another sword, Vivian thought. *Maybe that's the link…*

"Is anything else missing?" she asked.

"I think so," she said, clearly dazed. "If…if there's anything else, I can't see that it's missing." She turned from the wall, her gaze sweeping across the room, looking for other absences that did not exist.

Vivian glanced at Sterling, a silent exchange passing between them. They had seen this before—the selective thievery, the precision. It wasn't random; it was targeted. Whoever had taken the sword, be it the florists or someone else, had known where to look for the sword.

"Is there anywhere else that thieves may find interesting?" Sterling asked.

"My jewelry, I suppose. But that's upstairs in my closet."

"Go have a look anyway," Vivian said.

As Amelia nodded and left the room, wringing her hands, Vivian's mind worked furiously. She stepped closer to Sterling, lowering her voice. "Four hits now," she said. "Two involved historic swords. This isn't about money—it's about collectors. Someone specific. I think we can officially narrow that list of collectors and dealers down now."

Sterling's brow furrowed, the cogs in his mind visibly turning. "A collector with a penchant for historical swords?"

"Seems like it," Vivian agreed, her brain already profiling the kind of person who would commission such thefts. "Someone with deep pockets and an interest in blades."

Vivian leaned against the wall, her arms folded. The meticulousness of the thieves nagged at her, a puzzle demanding to be solved. A collector, yes, but also someone who understood the thrill of the hunt, the allure of possession. And someone who would have no qualms with sending out killers to get his treasures.

Sterling took his phone out and began composing a text. Noticing Vivian looking at him, curious, he looked up while texting and said,

“I’m going to update the list we sent out earlier…tell the teams compiling the list of dealers and collectors to home in on swords or historically relevant weapons.”

Vivian's mind raced. The George Washington short sword—gone. A symbol of power and history, now in the hands of a thief with taste for the unique. She thought about Jenna Caldwell, her stern face etched in her memory from the briefings. Professional, discreet, the kind of person who could slip in and out unnoticed.

"Jenna may have the answers we need," Vivian said, her eyes narrowing as she considered the implications.

Sterling glanced at her, his expression serious. "What are you thinking?"

"Jenna was here," Vivian replied, her voice firm with conviction. "Mrs. Hankins confirmed this. Jenna is canvassing these places. If we can figure out where else she's been, it might lead us to other potential targets—or even better, to our thieves. And it’s information we can get without having to interrogate her further."

"Right," Sterling nodded. “We can cross reference these collectors and sellers…see if *they* have had any contact or business with Jenna Caldwell.”

“And that does all sound boring, but it *could* give us the answers we need.”

Sterling nodded excitedly as he wrapped up his text. Just before he sent it, Amelia returned through the door. Her breath was slightly labored from rushing to and from her bedroom.

"My jewelry is all there,” she said. “Nothing else has been stolen."

"Thank you, Mrs. Hankins,” Vivian said. “Would you happen to—”

She was interrupted as another person came rushing to the office. It was the same FBI agent as before—the one with the startingly black eyes.

"Sterling," he said. "We just got a ping that some local blues have spotted Liam Wright's van.. They're keeping their distance until you arrive, nut said if it comes down to it, they have no problems overtaking him."

“Perfect,” Sterling said, already hurrying for the door. Vivian followed, feeling as if she’s been lobbed into a hurricane and was being buffeted about. “Got an address?”

“Sending it to you now, but, of course, it’s likely to change. I’ll also send you the contact info on the cops so you can keep up with them.”

Vivian hurried along behind Sterling. As they climbed the stairs back to the main floor, he peered back over his shoulder for just a moment. “You doing okay back there, Fox?”

“Yeah. It’s just...Jesus, this is fast paced.”

“It *can* be. But it’s better than all that waiting around, right?”

“Absolutely,” she said.

And with that, they made their way to the front door and stepped back out into the sunlight where the day had somehow arched its way beyond noon and, hopefully, was starting to lead them to the end of this case.

CHAPTER EIGHTEEN

Vivian still felt as if she was being tossed about by some unpredictable force of nature as she sat in the passenger seat of a sedan that was starting to feel far too familiar. The car's engine growled under Sterling's direction, the man himself a portrait of controlled haste. Vivian, however, found her thoughts snagging multiple threads, as always.

She wondered if this was another huge difference in their professions—Sterling's agent-oriented mind always laser-focused on the task at hand while her brain, trained for breaking into secret places unseen, tried to analyze about ten different things at once.

"Jenna Caldwell," she said, looking out into the thick clog of New York traffic. It was 3:35 in the afternoon now, and things were getting quite crowded out on the streets and sidewalks. "We need to dig into her past employments. She's the common denominator at every scene, and I have a hunch that's where we'll find our leverage."

"Agreed, but remember that cleaners like Jenna often get paid off the books. It's going to be like finding a needle in a haystack. I guarantee you that Amelia Hankins likely wouldn't have remembered had she not done business with her just three days ago."

In her mind's eye, she could see Jenna's stern features, the kind that betrayed nothing, that would keep secrets locked tight behind sharp eyes. Vivian knew that world well—the silence, the shadows, the currency of anonymity. But she also knew that everyone left traces, intentional or not.

The car lurched forward as Sterling took advantage of an opening in traffic, the cityscape around them blurring into streaks of color and light. Vivian let out a slow breath, trying to still the drumbeat of anticipation. God, how did FBI, Interpol, CIA, and their ilk tolerate all of this waiting and hoping? Each second felt like a drop falling into a pool of potential breakthroughs or backslides. It was maddening.

Up ahead, she saw a cop car, marked with a 223 on the back—the unit they were looking for. The unit that had been trailing Liam Wright.

Sterling had placed his phone on the center console, with the number of the policeman who was tailing Liam Wright already pulled up. He pressed Call, and it was answered on the second ring.

"This is Officer Bentz."

“Bentz, it’s Sterling. I see you just up ahead. You just passed the subway entrance on the right. You still got the van I your sight?

“Roger that.”

“Let me know if he turns off. I’m going to slowly make my advance and pass you when I can.”

“Sounds like a plan. There’s another car about two blocks over, ready to come in at an angle to block the van off if you need it.”

“Perfect. Thanks for the help. You mind staying behind us after I pass in case we need backup?”

“Not at all,” Bentz said with a little flicker of excitement in his voice.

Vivian can almost feel the raw energy as Sterling manages to inch closer and closer to Unit 223. Not wanting to alert Wright with sirens and lights, Sterling can only rely on his deft driving and the occasional good fortune in the left lane.

And then there was the van—a black rectangle bobbing in traffic roughly four car-lengths in front of Bentz’s Unit 223. It took another two minutes before Sterling can overtake Bentz, using a dicey maneuver at a flashing yellow light at a crosswalk. Sterling got a few middle fingers and cries of outrage but he didn’t even flinch.

Sterling adds some speed, nearly colliding with the back of a cab and then jerking the car suddenly to the right. Coming up on the left side of the van, Vivian can now see the sideview mirror.

"New York City isn’t really the best place for a high-speed chase, is it?” Vivian asked.

“Not at all…despite what movies might suggest. That’s why I plan on simply getting in front of him and stopping.”

“Oh. Well, I guess that works. Not as exciting, but…”

He smirked at her from behind the wheel as he pulled in closer to the van. Just one car separated them now, and despite the sluggish pace of it all, Vivian couldn't deny the little spike of adrenaline.

The van gave a right-turn signal as they approached a light. When the van turned, so did Sterling. The van lumbered around the corners like an old dog chasing its tail. It was there that Sterling decided to make his move. He cut in front of a delivery truck that was also taking the turn, coming so close to sideswiping it that Vivian had to bite back a cry of warning.

In the lane beside the van, Sterling slammed on the gas, quickly closing in the space of roughly thirty feet of empty lane ahead of them. The driver of the van—Liam Wright, presumably—looked out to him as they passed. Vivian, on the passenger side and closest to the driver as they passed, got a good look at him before Sterling overtook the van. The driver appeared to be rather young, surely no older than thirty. He had long, scraggly hair that hung to the sides of his head, blonde and curly. When he looked over to them, his eyes were wide with anger and surprise, perhaps feeling that he was just one errant jerk of a wrist away from an accident.

Vivian was jerked out of her study of him when Sterling finally started blasting on the horn, alerting the drivers in front of him. There was still about twenty feet of open space, but it was closing quickly as Sterling sped up to cut in front of the van. Vivian was accustomed to high-speed chases, having been involved in a few of them in order to elude capture in the past. But never in traffic like this. So when Sterling finally jerked the wheel hard to the right to swerve in front of the van, Vivian couldn't help but close her eyes and simply pray for the best.

She uttered a curse as the sedan came to a shuddering stop, angled awkwardly across two lanes. Within just a few seconds, horns began to blare from behind them as the intrusion was instantly blocking already-busy traffic.

No sooner had Vivian righted herself in her seat, realizing that they'd somehow managed to avoid a collision, Sterling was getting out of the driver's side. Vivian reached for her door handle but realized it would do no good. The van's driver's side front bumper was less than a foot away from her door. She could *maybe* open the door and have enough room to squeeze out, but she doubted it.

So she could only sit there for a moment as Sterling made his way quickly around the back of the car and hurried to the driver's side door of the van. Feeling a bit like an idiot, Vivian ambled over the center console and also got out on the driver's side. As her feet touched the pavement, she heard police sirens approaching, either coming to their aid or to make sure traffic didn't become an enormous mess.

"Out of the van!" Sterling commanded, showing his badge through the driver's side window. He hadn't drawn his sidearm yet, but Vivian saw that his right hand was hovering over it.

The driver's eyes were wide with a. whole new emotion now—fear. His ands went up almost robotically and then he realized he needed one of them to open his door. When the door opened, he nearly stumbled out of the van, his eyes darting around in the chaos of blaring horns, angry pedestrians, and the wailing sirens from nearby cop cars.

"Jesus, man," the drive said. "What's this about? Who are you—"

"Are you Liam Wright?" Sterling asked.

"Yeah…why? What do you think I've done?"

"We just want to talk, Liam," Vivian says, though her eyes were hard, unyielding.

"But not here, obviously, Sterling said. "Get in our car, Mr. Wright."

"But I—"

"Do it now, of your own accord, or you can do it in handcuffs," Sterling interrupted.

"What about the van?"

"I'll get it out of the way," Vivian said.

"Fine," Liam spat, his tone indicating it was anything *but* fine. He nodded curtly and allowed Sterling to lead him to the backseat of their car.

"Park it along that street," Sterling said, nodding to the one-way street to their right. "The first space you can find, please. I'll pick you up."

Vivian nodded and got behind the wheel of the van. As she shifted into drive and started to move it out of the street—careful not to strike too-eager drivers and pedestrians wo were trying to get around impatiently—she also did her best to take mental notes of the vehicle. It was mostly clean, and she could see no obvious signs of anything illegal, no tell-tale signs of violence.

But as she brought the van to the first parking spot she saw, she took a deep breath and picked up a faint but unmistakable scent. A fragrant mix of roses and lilies filled the confined space, stubbornly clinging to the air.

Quite a number of flowers had been inside this van at some point in the day.

So it appeared they had the right van. The question that remained was what role the driver played in the group she and Sterling had been chasing.

CHAPTER NINETEEN

Vivian felt the first true pangs of exhaustion as she observed Liam Wright from the opposite side of the table. They were back in another interrogation room with yet another suspect. It was exciting because, for all they knew, they now had three members of the murderous thieves in custody. But that excitement and all of the adrenaline she'd been feeling was causing her to crash a bit—not helped at all by the abbreviated amount of sleep from the night before.

The overhead lights cast harsh shadows over Liam's hunched figure. He sat at the bare metal table, his large hands clenched into fists, his knuckles whitening under the strain. He'd pushed the long, scraggly hair behind his ears, making him look even younger.

"Mr. Wright, I have to thank you for taking the easy route on this" Sterling said as he settled into the only other chair in the room, pulling it over to the table. Vivian admired the cool detachment he maintained, even though she could sense his underlying anticipation. "Could you tell us what time you delivered flowers to Mrs. Amelia Hankins' house today?"

Liam's head snapped up, his eyes wide and rimmed with red, the whites stark against his sallow skin. "I... I didn't deliver any flowers today." His voice wavered, betraying his composure.

"You're certain about that?"

"Yeah, absolutely certain."

"The van sure did *smell* like flowers," Vivian commented.

Sterling pulled up the screenshots he'd texted himself from Amelia Hankins' phone. He then slid the phone across the table toward Liam. The images depicted crisp images of Liam's van outside the Hankins' residence, a van identical to the one they had just chased down. Watching Liam's reaction, Vivian caught a flicker of something unexpected—an almost gleeful recognition.

"Oh, I see the confusion now," Liam said, leaning back in his chair, which creaked under his bulk. "You see, I sometimes rent my vans out. It's a side gig." His admission hung in the air, thick with implications.

"People pay good money for a bit of... discretion. That's why I charge them so much."

"Vans? Plural?" Sterling's eyebrow quirked up.

"Yep," Liam chuckled dryly, a crackling sound void of humor. But Vivian could see in his face that he knew he was likely on the verge of getting out of whatever trouble he may have been in. "Got another one just like it. They're both pretty popular for freelance delivery work."

"Freelance delivery of illegal goods, you mean?" Sterling prodded, his tone remaining even.

Liam shrugged, his muscular shoulders rolling beneath the thin fabric of his orange jumpsuit. "I don't ask questions, so long as they pay upfront. Keeps things simple. But I'm not naïve…so yeah, I think sometimes there's illegal stuff being moved."

Vivian felt a cold shiver travel down her spine. She knew this type of criminal—opportunistic, detached from the consequences of their actions. He could plead ignorance to the deeds of those who rented the vans and o tony make himself feel better, but could also keep himself from getting into any real legal trouble.

As she watched Liam's defiant display, she sensed that while he might not be directly responsible for the murder, he was certainly entangled in the web that led to it. And to her…that was just as bad. It was a strange and alien concept to her, having lived the last few years as a dedicated thief.

"Who rented the van this morning, Liam?" Sterling asked. "And what for?"

"Wait…I mean, am I in trouble here?" Liam asked, still looking conflicted.

"You sure as hell could be. It depends on how helpful you are."

Liam considered his options for a second before answering. "The guy didn't give me a real name. Told me to call him Lionheart. I was expecting my van to reek of something foul when he returned it, but it smelled like flowers. Weird, right?"

"And what did you charge for this Lionheart character to use the van?"

"Two grand for a two-hour joyride." He let out a short, mirthless laugh.

"Two thousand dollars cash, just like that?" Sterling probed, maintaining eye contact with Liam, searching for any flicker of deceit.

"Yep, cash. No names, no receipts. That's how these clients like it." Liam's gaze held steady, but Vivian thought she saw the slightest glimmer of guilt in them.

"Can you describe him?" Vivian asked. "This Lionheart character?"

"Late forties, I'd say. Guy had this handsome look about him, you know? Grey at the temples, the sort of guy older age looks good on." Liam squinted slightly as if trying to bring a clearer image of the man into focus.

"Accent?" Sterling interjected, his interest piqued.

"Accent..." Liam's eyes darted to the side, thinking. "Yeah, he had one. Not quite sure if it was British or maybe Irish. It was subtle, but definitely from that side of the pond."

"Did you notice anything else about him?" Vivian pushed.

"Nothing much. But the way he carried himself—confident, you know? Like he didn't have a care in the world."

"Handsome, greying, possibly British or Irish," Sterling recited, writing the details down. "And he paid in cash, so we can't trace it."

"Right," Liam confirmed.

"Thank you, Liam," Sterling said. "You'll have to stay here a bit longer for us to confirm all of this. An agent will be in soon to get alibis for the next few nights. But so long as you've been honest with us, I don't think you'll be in too much trouble here."

Sterling left the interrogation room, Vivian following closely behind. She glanced back at Liam and could see a bit of relief in his posture. She figured if he was guilty, he might still be agitated with the idea of more people coming to speak with him. Still, even if Liam wasn't one of the members of the group they were after, they now had another piece of the puzzle—even if it was as useless and flimsy as the moniker *Lionheart.*

"That name mean anything to you?" Sterling asked. "Lionheart?"

"No. But thieves working in groups often use codenames. Sometimes, their partners don't even know their actual names. It's a good way to make sure you keep yourself safe." Then, smiling, she added: "It makes me wonder how Caldwell and Belmont would react to hearing the name out of our mouths."

Sterling chuckled and clapped his hands together a single time. "That's damn good thinking, Fox."

Their attention turned further down the hall toward the other interrogation rooms. They found Jenna and Marcus still occupying the same room, still wearing the same sullen expressions as before. Vivian could almost smell their fear mingling with the stale coffee scent that lingered in the hallway. They entered Jenna's room first. She looked tired more than anything, and Vivian wondered if this might work in their favor.

"Your little operation is unraveling," Vivian started without preamble. "We found the van your team used this morning."

"What van?" Jenna asked.

Interesting that she didn't bother correcting me about an operation, Vivian. *Not a confession, but pretty close.*

"Used to deliver flowers, rented from a fellow in an interrogation room just down the hallway."

Belmont sat across from her, his silver hair catching the light in a way that seemed almost regal. His lips were a flat line, giving nothing away. "And I suppose you're going to tell me that finding a van is enough to pin anything on me?" he asked, his voice dripping with disdain.

"Depends on what you're willing to share," Sterling replied coolly, playing along with the ruse. "The person who rented this van called himself Lionheart. Ring any bells?"

Jenna's eyes flickered momentarily, a crack in her otherwise stoic facade. Belmont shifted in his chair, the faintest glint of fear in his eyes. But neither said a word, choosing to swallow whatever information they held.

"Time's running out for both of you," Vivian warned, letting her words hang heavy in the room. "Better to be a witness than a defendant, don't you think?"

For just the briefest of moments, Vivian thought Belmont was going to talk. But in the end, he simply inhaled deeply and shook his head. That was fine with Vivian. If *she'd* seen the recognition and slight alarm in their eyes at the mention of Lionheart, surely Sterling had. Even by being stubborn, the duo was pinning themselves closer and closer to the group.

"Have it your way," Sterling said, giving a half-hearted little wave as he headed back for the door.

Back out in the hallway, Sterling allowed himself a moment to lean against the wall and collect his thoughts. "So now," he said, "we narrow that list down. Antiques dealers and collectors with a penchant for expensive blades."

"Right," Vivian agreed.

Sterling seemed happy enough with that approach as they headed back down the hall, but Vivian couldn’t help but feel slightly defeated. More hunting, more digging, more hoping. At some point, there *had* to be more action, right? She'd gotten a taste of it when Sterling had cornered Liam in the van, but surely that couldn't be it.

Not as long as the killers are still out there, she thought. And with that nugget tucked away, she followed along with Sterling, hoping for another lead in whichever location the case led them to next.

CHAPTER TWENTY

He slipped into the antiques store like a shadow on a moonless night. The scent of polished wood and musty pages from ancient books filled his nostrils as he pretended to admire a gilded mirror that had seen more history than he ever would. He was irritated, pissed, even. A vein throbbed in his temple as he tried to keep his cool. Jasmine should have been there, casing the joint with her keen eye for detail, but she'd vanished off the grid—probably got herself and her dimwitted boyfriend pinched.

The bell above the door jingled incessantly as patrons shuffled in and out, their footsteps creaking on the wooden floorboards. The proprietor seemed to constantly be in motion, attending customers with an almost frantic energy, oblivious to the predator in their midst.

His gaze swept over the trinkets and baubles, but his mind was elsewhere; it was fixed on the prize that lay hidden within these walls—a small dagger with a history steeped in blood, used in Mayan ceremonies. But again…he was not accustomed to canvassing the places they were to it. He'd not been properly trained and honestly had no idea why Lionheart and Codex had sent him to do Jasmine's job.

He could almost feel the cool touch of the dagger's hilt in his palm, the weight of centuries-old secrets it carried. His group had been after this particular piece for months, ever since the owner had nearly auctioned it off for a fortune. Three million dollars. And from what he knew of Lionheart's expertise, they'd likely be able to fetch closer to five million for it.

As he feigned interest in a set of antique scales, his eyes scanned the shop for cameras, exits, and potential hiding places for the safe where the dagger would undoubtedly be secured. He memorized the layout with the precision of a man whose life depended on knowing every inch of his environment because, in a way, it did.

He imagined the blade glinting in the dim light, chiseling out hearts in the Mayan ceremonies. And yet, as he pictured himself wielding it, a different kind of edge crept into his craving—the razor-sharp thrill of taking a life, the power of playing God.

"May I help you with something?" the proprietor asked, pulling him back from the brink of his dark reverie.

"Just looking," he replied, his voice steady, betraying none of the turmoil that raged within him. "Your collection is... fascinating."

"Ah, thank you. Looking for anything in particular?"

"No, just having a look around."

"Well, let me know if you change your mind." And with that, the proprietor was off to chat with another patron.

He spent another five minutes looking at the store, getting a mental blueprint and marking off all areas of interest. His gaze slid across the contours of the hallway, its shadowy embrace hinting at secrets. The route to the office was clear in his mind, the map etched behind his eyelids. Turning on his heel, he made for the exit with a practiced nonchalance. The cool air outside greeted him, a stark contrast to the musky scent of antiquity that clung to his clothes.

As he left the store, he allowed himself a small smile. Soon, another story would unfold—one final heist before heading back home. Before he could return to Essex and sleep for days.

But deep down, he knew the truth. It wasn't just the dagger he coveted; it was the act itself, the ultimate assertion of control. The hunger was growing, and he's stopped trying to calm it. He had started to care more about the bloodshed rather than the job itself—and he wasn't quite sure how to feel about that.

The first murder had been hard. An older woman, and she'd actually been an eyewitness. He hadn't meant to kill her. But when his fit had slammed into her mouth in a warning shot, something inside of him had risen, had woken up. And when he saw her blood and shattered teeth, he punched again. And again and again. He'd continued punching the woman in the face even after he knew she was dead. And he would have kept going it if Lionheart hadn't pulled him away.

The second time, there had been two of them. Two drunk women in Ireland. He'd dispatched the first one easily enough. A simple stan wound to the heart. But the second one...he'd tried the same ting but his aim had been off. He'd let her suffer a bit and experiment on places to cut to see what hurt the most. And in that moment, the thing that had stirred awake in him during that first job had grabbed the controls and taken over.

He could feel it even now as he stepped out into the street. Outside, the street buzzed with the energy of the city. He hated New York. God, he wished he'd just opted out of this project...these five heists in this wretched city. But the payout…yeah, that would make it worth it. A cool one and a half million would be a—

His attention was snared as his eyes briefly glanced by an art studio window across the street. A woman was standing there, slightly blurred from the glass…but he was able to see enough. A red-haired beauty with an ocean of art situated behind her. And just like that, the world shrank away until nothing existed beyond the pane of glass separating them.

His heartbeat quickened, the rhythm syncing with the pulse of newfound obsession. She was the embodiment of every dark urge, a temptation to those darker urges he was growing tired of fighting against. The dagger and the wealth it promised all faded into insignificance.

Compelled as if by some primal force, Daniel found himself crossing the street. He felt like he was on a self-propelled conveyor belt, unaware of the movements of his legs as he found himself stepping beneath the awning of the art studio. He opened the door and the door chimed in his arrival. He let out a breath he wasn't aware he'd been holding.

Inside, the scent of oil paint and turpentine mingled with the faint odor of wood varnish. A quick glance around told him that this wasn't so much a studio as it was a small art gallery that dealt in restorations. The red-haired woman who'd so ensnared him was behind a small desk, working on restoring a rather old oil painting.

She turned, her eyes locking onto his, and he felt the words clog in his throat, suffocated by the sudden onslaught of need. His silence wasn't one of awe or reverence; it was the heavy quiet before the storm. He could see it play out—the grip, the struggle, the surrender. It was all there, tantalizingly close within his imagination.

She would be next. He'd already killed once today—the woman int e laundry room of the mansion. But he felt the urge again, like electricity crackling in his fingers as he looked at the woman with the cleaning brush behind the desk.

Her movements were fluid, hypnotic, as she adjusted the frame. She was real, tangible, not just an image glimpsed through glass. Daniel's hands ached with the effort of restraint, his veins surging with the promise of what was to come.

He cleared his throat, trying to appear normal, but every fiber of his being screamed in resistance. This wasn't about blending in anymore; it was about the thrill, the power, the control. But she was looking at him, and he couldn't stand out. He needed to appear like a normal man who'd just stepped in off the street.

"Your brushwork is remarkable," Daniel managed to rasp out, his voice foreign to his own ears. It was the sound of a man barely holding on to his civility, a veneer so thin it could be shattered with a breath.

The woman looked up, her smile a mix of pride and fatigue. "Oh, thank you. I'm just finishing up some restoration on this old piece." She gestured at the canvas—a riot of colors that spoke of an age long past—a glimpse of an old, rural yard with three children at play. Her fingers held the frame gently, lovingly, and Daniel found himself imagining those hands growing limp, the light in her eyes dimming into nothingness.

"Art restoration, huh?" he prodded, feigning interest while his mind spun with darker thoughts.

"Yes, I've been doing it for years now. There's something about bringing old art back to life... almost like reversing time." Andrea's voice held a note of wistfulness that echoed strangely in Daniel's skull.

"Are you an artist yourself?" she asked, unaware of the tempest brewing just beneath his calm exterior.

"Something like that," Daniel muttered, his gaze never leaving her face. He studied the contours of her form, the rise and fall of her chest with each breath. She was beautiful, yes, but it was the prospect of extinguishing that beauty that held his attention.

The vibration in his pocket jolted him from his reverie. Lionheart. The name flashed across the screen before he silenced it. The call tethered him to reality, to the reason why he was supposed to be here in the first place. But the dagger, the heist, they all paled in comparison to the masterpiece before him—a life waiting to be snuffed out by his hand.

He smiled politely and stepped away from the desk. He made his way back outside, the cool air of the evening doing little to quell the fire inside him. A slight drizzle of rain was falling as the phone kept ringing, and he chose to ignore it. As he walked away, he made a silent promise—to return, to claim the life that danced so tantalizingly close to the edge.

He saw her eyes and her red air sharply in his mind as he kept his eyes open for an available cab to take him to his room.

His rented room was a haven of sorts, a nondescript box in a seedy hotel where no one asked questions. The place reeked of bleach and desperation, but it was perfect for someone who didn't want to be found. Per Lionheart's instructions, all three of them had booked rooms at different locations—just another form of safety and precaution. As for Jasmine and Gollum, they'd been their contacts here in New York, so they'd simply lived where they'd always lived.

And look at the now, he thought as he flagged down a cab. *Gone. Ghosts. Useless.*

The cab approached and when he got inside, the Mayan dagger and tonight's heist were the last things on his mind. All he could think of was the woman from the studio, how she held the brush, and how she had no idea whatsoever that she'd not live to see another sunrise.

CHAPTER TWENTY ONE

Vivian's breath fogged up the glass as she peered into yet another dimly lit shop, its windows crowded with the silhouettes of swords and armor from ages past. The door chimed mournfully behind her as she stepped out onto the sidewalk, Sterling right on her heels. They exchanged a glance that carried the weight of their frustration—another dead end.

"Three shops down," she muttered, pulling her coat tighter around her as a shield against the growing chill brought in by the rain. "Nothing to show for it."

Sterling's eyes were on the horizon, where the city bled into the overcast sky. "We keep at it," he said, his voice steady despite the setback. "The list will come through eventually."

As they walked back to where they'd parked the sedan, the clouds above seemed to close in, suffocating what little light the afternoon had left.. Sterling unlocked the car, and they slid inside, the rain pattering softly against the roof.

With no fresh leads to propel them, Vivian and Sterling had started looking into some of the shops on the expansive list themselves while waiting for a narrowed-down version from the bureau. Vivian could tell that Sterling viewed it as little more than grunt work, but she respected him for not griping about it and setting out to get the job done no matter how demeaning the task.

"Never thought I'd miss the simplicity of an art heist," Vivian said wryly, watching the rain streak down the windshield.

Sterling chuckled, the sound oddly comforting amidst the drumming rain. "You're not just a thief anymore, Fox. You've got potential as an agent," he said, turning to face her. "So…you ready tell me yet?"

"Tell you what?"

"What made you want to join the FBI when you were younger?"

She glanced at him, surprised by the question. It wasn't like Sterling to probe into personal history—a feeling based on the grand total of two days she'd known him. He'd asked this question before, but things were different now—even though it had been a short period of time.

And quite honestly, she wasn't sure if she was comfortable getting into such things with him. Surprisingly, though, she found herself willing to talk about it, if for no other reason than filling the time between shop visits. The gentle rhythm of the rain seemed to slow time, loosening tongues and defenses alike.

"I wanted to make a difference," she said after a moment, her voice softer than she intended. "To stop people from hurting others. To be on the right side of the law for once."

Sterling nodded and made an *mm-hmmm* noise. “No offense, but that's a canner answer. What's the *real* reason?”

She looked out at the rain-blurred city. The drizzle drummed on the roof of the sedan like odd music. Vivian watched the raindrops race each other down the window, their chaotic paths mirroring her thoughts.

"When I was young," Vivian began, her voice barely rising above the rain's patter, "a kid from my neighborhood vanished. For nine weeks, this eight-year-old girl was gone. Taken from her family, just vanished into thin air, you know? It was as if she'd been swallowed by the earth. Posters plastered everywhere, candlelight vigils the whole thing. My parents visited with the girl's parents, and they were just….just *miserable*. Then, one day, the FBI found her." She paused, the memory vivid as lightning in her mind's eye. "They brought her back to a family that had almost lost hope. I remember the joy and how complete that family looked after that. And when it was all over, I just held the FBI in this godlike esteem."

Vivian glanced at Sterling, gauging his reaction. His face was stoic, yet his eyes held a flicker of understanding. “That makes a good deal of sense,” he said. “It's a pretty common story, too. Nit the kidnapping, but cadets and recruits talking about some moment in their life with the cops or the FBI made some huge impact on them.”

“Yeah, well…that's what drew me to the idea of the FBI—before my life took...other turns. Now…your turn then. What about you? What led you to become an agent?"

Sterling's gaze lingered on the street outside before returning to her. "Tradition, for starters. My father served in the military, and so did my grandfather. I joined the British forces, continuing the lineage. Nothing too complex or exciting."

"From soldier to Interpol agent," Vivian observed.

"Indeed," Sterling replied. "When the opportunity arose to join Interpol, it seemed like the right step forward. The scope of work, the complexity of cases—it was a new challenge. And I've always been one to chase after a challenge."

"Never looked back?" Vivian asked.

"Not a single time," he confirmed, a smile tugging at the corner of his lips despite their grim situation. "Just two weeks ago, I was in Greece working on a case all by my lonesome and now where I am in rainy NYC with you. It's a pretty unpredictable job. I love it."

Vivian nodded, considering his words. In the world of law enforcement, they were both driven by a common goal—justice. Yet the roads they had taken were as divergent as the raindrop trails on the glass. She felt a newfound respect for Sterling, not just as an agent, but as someone who was dedicated to righting wrongs and helping those in need.

"Well, for what it's worth," she said, "I think you were a pretty good fit for a lady's first experience as an Interpol tag-along."

"Thanks…I think."

The good-natured comradery was broken up by the ringing of Sterling's phone. They both went quiet at once and things felt tense again Vivian had started to view the ringing of Sterling's phone as a potential warning bell of sorts—that there was a new lead or that the killer thieves had struck again.

He answered the phone, pressing it to his ear. "Sterling speaking."

Vivian's gaze lingered on the droplets tracing paths down the windshield as she listened to Sterling's very brief and clipped end of the conversation. He hung up less than ten seconds after answering, and he looked a bit more excited.

"Our friends at the Bureau are sending over a list of dealers and collectors," he said. "They've narrowed it down according to those who hold swords, knives, any sort of blade. It should be hitting my inbox any minute now."

She leaned over to peek at the screen as an email notification pinged. Sterling opened up the email, tapped on the attachment, and the list popped open in front of them. Vivian did a quick count and was surprised to see only fifteen names.

"Not as daunting as I expected," Vivian admitted, scanning the list. "But it's still going to be a needle in a haystack."

"Then let's start sifting," Sterling replied, his fingers already dancing across the screen to map out their next move.

As they prepared to dive into the search once more, another call interrupted their planning. Sterling's face grew serious as he listened, nodding occasionally. Vivian felt a ping of panic. So many calls in such a little time…eventually, one of these calls were going to be bad news. Another body, another hit.

She again listened to one side of a conversation, feeling slightly left out. All of Sterling's responses were just one or two words, and she couldn't out together the context. After a minute or so, he gave one final response.

"Understood," he said tersely before ending the call.

"New development?" Vivian inquired, feeling the familiar surge of adrenaline that accompanied unexpected leads.

"Potentially," Sterling responded, his eyes narrowing slightly. "NYPD just got a report from a worried husband. His wife isn't answering her phone, hasn't been seen since leaving work. And there was mention of a suspicious individual around her workplace."

"Doesn't necessarily connect to our case," Vivian pointed out, although the coincidence nagged at her.

"True, but given that we have no new leads and only a list to go by at the moment, we should take what we can get," Sterling said, starting the engine. "We're heading to the studio where she works. He shrugged and added, "It's likely nothing. A domestic squabble or overworked imagination. But there's another coincidence to this…"

"Which is?"

"The studio in question is directly across the street from one of the stores on our list. Regal Antiquities and Heirlooms. *And* the owner of the studio told the police that he did recall a strange individual in the shop earlier in the day...a creepy bloke that seemed smitten with this missing woman."

"That *does* make things a bit more interesting."

"So I think that shop is our next stop," Sterling said. "And if it's all for naught, then at least we can knock one of those locations off of our list. Now, as for this art studio, do you want to run a quick search for it online, give us some insights into the place?"

"Sure."

She did as he asked while Sterling pulled back out onto the street and headed in the direction of the shop. Vivian found the shop's website easily enough. There wasn't much information on it, other than the fact that they collected and restored "priceless works of art and other family treasures." There was an option to make an appointment for sales or appraisals. And the hours of operation were a bit odd. It was not the sort of place that held regular nine-to-five hours.

"I've got it right here, but the hours are weird. Eleven to three today. They're closed."

"Is there a number for after-hours?"

She poked around the website and shook her head after a moment. "Sure is. Right here. Cody Aldridge."

"Call it, would you? With any luck, Aldridge is the owner. Let him know you're with Interpol and that it's imperative that we speak to him."

"Okay," she said, typing the number in. "I think it would be more effective coming for a male with a British voice, but okay…"

This got a smile out of him, but it was brief. He was too caught up in the whirlwind of the moment to feel anything other than a sense of duty, she supposed. As the phone rang in Vivian's ear, she felt it, too. They'd gone from having no leads to suddenly having multiple irons in the fire in less than five minutes. It was almost intoxicating, and as she spoke to the owner of Regal Antiquities and Heirlooms, she couldn't help but feel that they were finally closing in on something…if not the end of the case then, at the very least, the final act.

CHAPTER TWENTY TWO

Vivian's eyes darted across the bustling café, its walls adorned with vintage French posters and trinkets. The aroma of freshly ground coffee beans mingled with the scent of buttery croissants, causing her to realize how hungry she was. She suddenly couldn't recall the last time she'd eaten.

The owner of the art studio, Cody Aldridge, had been running errands when Vivian called him and they'd made plans to meet at a halfway point—the little French bistro she and Sterling were currently stepping into. They spotted Aldridge easily enough, dressed in the pinstripe suit he'd described to her on the phone. He was sitting by a window, sipping leisurely on a coffee.

As she and Sterling approached, she could sense the man's unease, the tension in his shoulders like coiled springs. Vivian sat down first, followed by Sterling. Aldridge eyed them carefully, as if he thought he might be dining with bears rather than other human beings.

"Mr. Aldridge," Vivian greeted, her voice low but firm as she slid into the seat opposite him. "Thank you for meeting us on such short notice."

"Of course," he replied, his voice slightly shaky. "I understand time is of the essence. And if I can help find Andrea, I want to help."

Sterling, taking the seat beside Vivian, nodded curtly. "We'll get straight to the point," he said, his British accent crisp and rigid against the café's hum of conversation. "The call from her husband was only two hours ago. So she'd nowhere near being considered a missing individual. Twenty-four entire hours have to pass for that to be the case. However, we're currently working on a case that makes us a little more interested in this situation."

"I see. So what do you need from me?"

"The policeman I spoke to said that when you were contacted and initially asked about Andrea's day, you mentioned a peculiar individual that came by the shop. Do you remember enough about him to give us details?"

Aldridge's eyes went glossy for a moment as he nodded and dug into his memories. "Yes, well, it was near closing…maybe an hour before I closed up shop. So I'd say two o'clock, give or take ten minutes." He began, licking his lips nervously, his hands trembling slightly along the cup of coffee. "This man... he wasn't like our usual clients. He lingered around Andrea's workspace, kept peering over as if he was looking for something—or someone."

"Can you describe him?" Vivian pressed.

"Average height, nondescript really, but his eyes..." Aldridge shuddered. "They were cold, calculating. He spoke briefly to Andrea. I didn’t hear the conversation but got the impression that he may have been trying to flirt but failed. I joked about it to Andrea, trying to lighten the mood. She shrugged it off, said the guy was harmless. But now..." His words trailed off, weighted by the gravity of the situation.

"Did they interact beyond that?" Sterling asked.

"No. Andrea said he commented on her brushwork and that was about it. She said he left rather quickly. His phone rang in his pocket and he got a bit skittish. Left right after his phone rang."

"Anything else you can remember might be critical," Vivian urged, her intuition buzzing like live wires. She locked eyes with Aldridge, willing him to recall even the smallest detail. “Anything at all.”

He shook his head, frustration etched into his furrowed brow. "That's all I can remember. But Andrea, like I said…she laughed it off at the end of the day, said she'd dealt with stranger folks."

“How about security footage?” Sterling asked. “Do you have security cameras in your studio?”

Aldridge nodded, a touch of apprehension in his eyes. "Yes, but I can't get to it until I'm home or at the shop. And home is much closer to where we currently are."

"Would you be able to go into the footage and see if you can get a good look at him?” Sterling asked. “I hate to ask, but it would be appreciated if it would be the very first thing you do when you get home.” Sterling then slid a business card across the table to Aldridge and said, “You can call the number on here.”

“Of course,” Aldridge said.

"One last thing," Vivian said. "By any chance, did you or Andrea happen to see this man come in or out of the antiques shop across the street, Regal Antiquities and Heirlooms?"

"Sorry…can't say that I did. And if Andrea saw such a thing, she didn't mention it."

Vivian and Sterling shared a glance, nodding solemnly to one another. “Thank you for your time, Mr. Aldridge.”

They got up to leave, making their way back through the bistro. When they were outside, the rain started coming down a bit harder. They remained under the bistro awning for a moment, gathering their thoughts.

“So what do you think?” Sterling asked.

Vivian eagerly wanted to give her thoughts, but she also felt like she was being tested…which she didn't appreciate. "I think if Andrea is missing, there's a good chance she may already be dead…and if she’s dead, I bet you anything her body is in Regal Antiquities and Heirlooms. It’s how they’ve operated the last few scenes, only…”

“Only what?” Sterling asked, coaxing it out of her.

“We need to find out if the antiques place is still open. If it is, I doubt the group was brazen enough to just roll up and steal it. And that’s another thing,” she said, a new idea suddenly coming to her.

“What?”

"While here on American soil, the first two heists were at night, under cover of darkness. But there was something about the way the one this morning unfolded at the Hankins house. Something about it felt rushed…like it was spurred about by opportunity. I bet you anything the original plan was to hit that study tonight and take the Washington sword. But we’ve got two of their members already. Maybe they’re getting scared and rushing things.”

“So maybe they *would* attack an antiques store in broad daylight?”

“Maybe. It would be irresponsible in terms of working a proper heist, but…”

“So let’s get in touch with Regal Antiquities and Heirlooms,” Sterling said.

“Didn’t the list the bureau sent have the numbers of the owners as well?”

“Sure did,” Sterling said, quickly reaching for his phone. He tapped and scrolled with quick precision as they stood under the bistro awning, not yet ready to brave the rain. As the phone began to ring, he surprised Vivian by placing the call on speaker mode. He held it slightly out in front of them so both of them could hear.

After three rings, a man with a refined and older sounding voice picked up. “Regal Antiquities and Heirlooms, this is Harold.”

“Hello, Harold,” Sterling said. “I’m an Interpol agent, working a local investigation. I’m sorry to tell you that your shop may be the target for a group of thieves…thieves that have a penchant for leaving at least one murdered body behind."

"Are you…I swear, if this is a prank, I'll—"

"It's not a prank. If you'd like, I can give you my badge number as well as the contact information for my director, Elise Garnett out of Lyon, France."

"Oh…okay, then. That's not necessary. A heist, you say? Here?"

"Perhaps," Sterling said. "Are you currently still at your shop?"

"No. I closed up half an hour ago. Is it happening *now?*"

"No, sir. I do have to ask you, though…a question about your inventory—specifically, do you carry any historically relevant weaponry? Swords, to be exact."

"As a matter of fact, I do. A Mayan blade, quite ancient and exceptionally rare. It's not something you'd find in just any collection."

"What can you tell me about it?"

"Well, it's believed to have been used in sacred ceremonies. It's made of obsidian, volcanic glass, sharper than you might think. Came to me via an estate sale, some old explorer's collection. It's been authenticated, of course. Quite the piece. But given its value, I keep it securely stored away in my safe. Had plans to offer it at auction one of these days."

"I see. And is your safe hidden away?"

"It's in my…wait. Hold on. Should I be concerned?" Harold's voice crackled through the phone, an undercurrent of unease threading his words.

"Not likely," Sterling said. "We have reason to believe your store will be targeted tonight or very soon after tonight. As such, we'll be keeping an eye on it in the hopes of tracking down this group of murderous thieves."

"Oh. I see."

The silence from Harold was palpable, a quiet acknowledgment. Vivian could picture him, the gears turning as he processed the looming threat. She imagined the pristine glass cases in his shop, each harboring treasures untold, and the Mayan blade silently waiting in the darkness of a safe.

"Understood," Harold finally replied. His voice had taken on a new edge—a mix of fear and resolve. "Can you please keep me informed?"

"Of course. And thank you for your help."

Sterling ended the call and let out a deep breath. “I know you seem to hate all the waiting around,” he said, looking at Vivian, but it looks like that’s the next step for right now.

“Staking out the antique shop?”

“Yes. And given your line of work, I’m sure you understand that we have to remain discreet. We need to stay hidden, giving the thieves no indication that we’re on to them.”

“And what about Andrea?” But she already knew the answer, and she didn’t like it much.

“We have to assume these madmen will stick to their usual schedule,” Sterling said. “And from what we can tell, the murder happens either during or immediately after the theft.”

“True. But have thy ever *taken* someone on advance?”

"We just don't know. There was one case in Paris where we think the person selected for the murder may have been taken about an hour before the heist, but we aren't sure. But everything we know about these bastards tells me that Andrea will be safe up until the heist. And by that time, we—"

“By that time, we’ll have the drop on them.”

“That’s the hope, yes,” Sterling said.

“Then let’s get moving.”

Together, they stepped out into the rain and hurried for the car. Vivian could feel a surge of adrenaline welling up, ready to tear through her. But she reminded herself that a woman’s life hung in the balance beyond capturing these thieves. And with that in her mind, this suddenly felt like the most important job of her career—not stealing something, but doing her best to preserve the most important thing of all: a life.

CHAPTER TWENTY THREE

Vivian's eyes were fixed on the antique store across the street, its windows dark now that night had properly fallen over the city. They'd parked discreetly, a vantage point chosen with tactical precision. Vivian had given the spot her seal of approval, having looked for hiding-in-plain-sight locations just like this one throughout her career.

Sterling had parked on the street over to the right, having placed a call to the city to inform them that an unmarked sedan would be blocking a fire hydrant and for the love of God, to not come writing tickets. From here, they could see the antique store's façade, the windows reflecting the ghostly dance of streetlights and neon signs. The store stood silent, unaware of the watchful eyes guarding it. However, they were far enough away and out of the main line of sight from the building that she didn't think the thieves would give their car a second glance.

"You ever done this before?" Vivian asked Sterling. "A stakeout, I mean."

"Oh, several. My record is six days, in a sweltering motel in Sierra Leone."

"Oh my God, what for?"

He smirked and said, "Sorry…classified. I can't tell you."

She smirked right back, fining that she was very interested to hear some of his stories. She knew that Interpol agents did quite a bit of traveling for their cases and she wondered just how many locations Sterling had been sent out to.

The night deepened around them, each passing minute ratcheting the tension higher. Vivian's gaze never wavered from the store across the street, her mind alert to every movement, every shadow. She tried to imagine herself in the position of the thieves, making sure she wasn't missing a small detail that may leave her and Sterling unaware. But as far as she could tell, she'd thought of everything.

She figured they'd go through the back because it was safer. But she also knew they'd have at least one person walk by the front—just to make sure there were no loiterers or roaming cops that would cause problems later.

To prepare for their stakeout, they'd opted for take-out subs for dinner. The gentle hum of the city faded into the background as Vivian took a bite of hers, the crunch of lettuce and savory taste of turkey momentarily distracting her from the task at hand.

Sterling, chewing methodically beside her, glanced at his watch, then at the phone lying between them. It buzzed, breaking the silence. He tapped the speaker button and said: "Sterling here."

"Sterling, this is Agent Donaldson, FBI. We've got the net in place two blocks to the east. Last I heard, three units from NYPD are closing it up to the east."

"Sounds perfect," Sterling said. "Thanks for the assist."

Sterling ended the call and is fingers drummed on the wheel, a soldier's rhythm to ward off the stillness. Vivian watched him, noting the subtle shift in his posture, the readiness that infused his being. He was in his element. He was ready to strike at a moment's notice; she could practically feel the energy coming off of him.

His phone rang again—the fourth time in under ten minutes. "This is Sterling," he answered, again setting it to speaker. Then, with a smile, he added, "And Fox."

"This is Deputy Carter," a woman's voice said. "Wanted you to know that we've got eyes on eleven of the fourteen shops you sent us, and units are on the way to surveil the other three. All should be in place within ten minutes."

"Good. Thanks for the heads up."

"You're quite popular tonight," Vivian said. "But it looks like you're used to this, huh?"

"A bit. No two jobs with Interpol are the same. Well, not usually."

Vivian looked out at the street again, her hands tightening around her sub. This was a different kind of anticipation than what she was used to, a different kind of heist. Once, she would have been on the inside, slinking through shadows, lifting treasures with a deft touch. Now, she was on the opposite side of things, and she still couldn't quite wrap her head around it.

Night wrapped around them like a cloak, and time stretching thin as they waited. Vivian felt the familiar itch, the urge to move, to act. But discipline held her still, her breaths slow and even. She knew the dance of shadows and light, the patient game of cat and mouse. Thief, detective, agent…it didn't matter. Patience was key in situations like this. She knew that better than anyone.

Once, she'd waited a day and a half outside of an old warehouse when a golden crown from the Victorian area was being transferred. She'd done that job alone, forever starting at the side of a warehouse just outside of Los Angeles. So she was no stranger to the waiting game. But something about this situation felt different, and not just because she was working with an Interpol agent.

The sub lay forgotten in her lap, her appetite lost to the growing tension. Each passing second was a thread pulled taut, ready to snap. They were close now, she could feel it. She had no doubt at all that the night would end with the rest of this group captured…and hopefully with Andrea being saved.

Vivian shifted in her seat, the leather creaking under her. Sterling was silent beside her, his eyes scanning the quiet street, the phone's soft glow illuminating his features. He really was quite handsome, and she'd always been a sucker for a guy with a British accent. In another life, maybe she would have tried to grab his attention to see if there was a spark between them.

It was a ridiculous notion, really. Her career had left no time for a true love life in any sense of the term. A few weekend flings here and there was all she's allowed time for. The idea of remaining serious with anyone seemed just as surreal as her current predicament—trying to capture thieves.

"Ever think about what you'll do after all this?" Sterling's voice cut through her thoughts, casual and soft.

She turned to him, considering the question. "After all *this?"* she asked, gesturing to the city in front of her. "You mean working with Interpol?"

"Yes."

"I haven't considered it," she said. Ah, but that was a lie. Less than forty-eight hours ago, she'd made plans to run away from Sterling and this case the first chance she for. But now…well, things were different now, having seen two of the innocent victims up close.

"You *should* consider it, you know. You're good at this. Better than some seasoned agents I know. You have a knack for it."

"Thanks."

She felt something creeping into her tongue…a fact about her past that she'd conveniently left out. The story she'd told him about the neighborhood girl going missing had been one hundred percent true.

But it hadn't been the only reason she's eyed the FBI as a career. There was more to it, a deeper and darker truth. But she'd only told one person about it before, and it had been hard—it had made her far too vulnerable. And she wasn't there with Sterling.

She swallowed it down before it had time to properly form. She checked the dashboard clock and saw that somehow, it had come to be 11:47. She'd forgotten how hard it was to keep proper track of time in New York when the lights were always on and the city seemed to always been wide open and alive.

When she looked away from the clock, she caught movement in the darkness and shadow along the edge of Regal Antiquities and Heirlooms. She leaned forward a bit just to make sure her eyes weren't growing weary and deceiving her.

"You see it, too, huh?" Sterling asked.

"Yeah, I see it."

A cab eased to a stop along the curb, just shy of the end of the block. The door opened, spilling weak light onto the pavement, silhouetting two figures that stepped out. They lingered for a moment in discussion before the vehicle pulled away, leaving them shrouded in the newfound darkness.

They stood there for a moment, huddled together. Because of the distance and the lack of proper lighting, it was difficult to judge their size or sex. After a few seconds, they began to move—first toward the back of the building and then back toward the front.

Sterling tensed beside her, staring. "Why the hell would master thieves take a cab to the place they're going to rob and then send it off?"

"That *is* strange," she said. "It also provides one more witness in the cab driver. And there's only two of them now. Weird. Unless…maybe they have a car somewhere nearby. That leaves two different cars to trace—the cab and whatever they're driving. It would make it hard to do any sort of search, especially if they ditch the getaway within five minutes of getting inside."

Sterling chuckled. "Given some thought to this stuff before, have you?"

She said nothing as they continued to watch the figures in the shadows. The air in the car felt charged and Vivian begam to sense that soon, it would carry them out it the night to follow the thieves.

Vivian's eyes narrowed, scrutinizing the movements of the two shadowy figures as they suddenly split up. The first slinked towards the back of the antique store, his gait casual but deliberate, blending into the backdrop of the quiet street. The second lingered at the storefront, peering through the display window in a casual manner before spinning on a heel, feigning disorientation, and then following suit - a clear signal to Vivian that these were no ordinary late-night browsers.

"Looks like we're up," Sterling's voice was soft but carried an edge of command as he tapped the side of his phone, and called the FBI agent who'd pinged him earlier. "Agent Donaldson, we've got movement...two figures that seem to be looking the exterior over. I feel like this is it. Would you mind informing the other corners of the net?"

"Roger that."

Sterling ended the call and reached for his door handle. Vivian stopped him before he could open it, though. "Wait."

"What?"

"If these *are* our thieves, we need to make sure they aren't going to come back to the front. If we run into them and spook them, that's going to make things far more difficult if we have to chase them down. Wait until they're out if sight and then given them about thirty seconds. If we catch them in the act, they're busted and have nowhere to run...especially not in such a small building."

He smiled widely at her and nodded. "Damn good thinking, Fox."

"It happens on occasion."

They watched as the second figure disappeared into the darkness behind the store. As Vivian and Sterling waited their thirty seconds, a group of four young, late-night partier walked by the car, either on their way home or to find another party-spot. Vivian ignored them completely, her eyes on the darkened shape of Regal Antiquities and Heirlooms.

"Alrighty," Sterling said. "That's thirty seconds. Let's move."

Without a sound, she and Sterling slipped from their car, the cold bite of wet, night air nipping at their skin. They moved with practiced stealth, shadows chasing shadows across the darkened street. The sounds of the city enveloped them but for a moment, walking as quietly as she could, Vivian felt like she might very well be walking on the moon.

They came to the store and then instantly slipped into the shadows along the side. Sterling kept the lead which was good; Vivian had become very much aware that she didn't have a weapon—not ideal, given the situation they were thrusting themselves into.

The back alley behind the antiques store was shrouded in gloom, the only light spilling from a flickering bulb above a rusted doorway. The noise from inside the store was muddled, but unmistakable to Vivian. The soft clatter of the tools of her trade being used, the dull thud of heavy steps on old wooden floors. They *were* being very quiet, but Vivian's ears had long ago been trained to hear such things, always aware of even her own slightest movement while on the job.

Sterling gestured to Vivian, two fingers pointing towards the rear entrance where the door hung askew, its lock defeated by more than a key. With a glance that communicated volumes, they advanced together. Vivian's pulse quickened, her senses sharpened by the prospect of what lay beyond the door.

In sync, Sterling stepped inside, and then Vivian. She looked to the lock and saw that there were clear signs of tampering, but the door and the frame itself were still pristine. In other words, these guys were good.

Not as good as her, but good.

The back door led to a small hallway and, almost immediately to the left, a restroom. The air was thick with the scent of old varnish and dust. Vivian's eyes had just begun to adjust to the dimness when the dark hallway ahead of her erupted into movement.. A figure lunged from the shadows, a rapid blur aimed squarely at Sterling. Sterling's reflexes were quick, but the assailant had not only a head start, but momentum. The figure collided with Sterling, and both bodies went to the ground with a heavy thud.

Vivian's mind became a silent metronome, starting to analyze each second as the attacker got to their feet. He threw out a punch, and Vivian saw it coming from a mile away. Not only was she able to block the strike, but she had a large opening and a clear target. She jettisoned out a hard right-handed jab that caught the attacker squarely in the chest. There was an *oof* sound as the attacker went stumbling back. As he did, he swung wildly, but Vivian deftly sidestepped, her own fist finding its mark again.

This time, she clocked him directly in the jaw. There was a click as his teeth snapped together, and a sudden jolt of electric pain up Vivian's arm. She hadn't thrown a punch in years outside of a gym, and she was afraid she may have injured her wrist from improper technique.

The man reeled again and this time he went to the floor. He started moving right away, but he looked like a fish that was struggling to understand why it was suddenly out of water. She figured he'd be out for at least a minute or so. As she looked down at him, it was the first time in the flurry of activity that she noticed he was wearing a generic, black ski mask.

Sterling got to his feet behind her, using the wall for support. He'd been hit in the head with something; a small trickle of blood was coming from his eyebrow, trickling down his cheek.

Remaining as quiet as she could, Vivian gave him a thumbs up with a questioning look on her face. He nodded and returned the gesture.

Without a word, they started walking toward the sound of movement in a room up ahead. The door was opened and a bright light shone out of it—not a lamp or an overhead, but probably some sort of flashlight to help with the picking of the lock on the safe. Vivian assumed this was Harold's office, the safe inside holding the Mayan dagger.

Through the opened door, Vivian glimpsed the other thief. If he'd heard any of the sounds from the fight out in the hallway, he made no such sign. And she supposed she understood it. The thief had already managed to break into the safe. He held the Mayan dagger in his hand, a mocking beacon of success. She burst into the room, the element of surprise on her side.

"It's beautiful, huh?" Vivian said.

The thief jumped in surprise, whirling around and nearly dropping the blade. He was also wearing a ski mask. And when he was fully facing her, she understood why his grip had not been the best.

He was also holding a gun. And it was aimed directly at her, its barrel less than four feet from her head. Time stuttered, crystallizing the moment, and Vivian simply waited for the blast to come—the blast that would end her life.

A blast did indeed come. And when she heard it, she was sure she was dead. Her heart even seemed to stop beating, as if accepting his fate a heartbeat too early.

It took another moment for her to understand that the gunshot hadn't come from in front of her, but from behind. Sterling had regained his footing and now stood in the doorway, his service weapon held out toward the thief.

Sterling had aimed high, taking the thief squarely in the shoulder. The thief's gun clattered to the floor as he stumbled back against the wall. Vivian exhaled sharply, her body trembling from the adrenaline that still coursed through her veins. A small part of her was till certain she was dead, that she was seeing all of this from outside of her body.

"You okay?" Sterling asked as he rushed past her and toward the thief.

"Yeah…yeah, I think so."

The thief began to groan from the floor, trying to pull himself up. But Sterling was on him at once, expertly cuffing him. Vivian noticed, though, that he was not cuffing the man's wrists together. Instead, he cuffed the thief to the arm of a chair to the right side of the room, tucked behind a desk. This, Vivian assumed, was presumably not to place any more stress or pain on the man's wounded shoulder.

"Are you Lionheart?" Sterling asked the man.

"Go to hell."

"Clever," Sterling bit back. "Where's Andrea?"

"What?"

As Sterling tried getting information out of the wounded man, Vivian looked back out into the hallway. The man she'd decked was starting to come around.

"Got another set of cuffs?" Vivian asked Sterling.

"Nope. If he comes to, and you have to, just knock him out again for all I care."

She nodded and stepped back out into the hallway. "Andrea?" she called out. "Andrea, are you here?"

She moved swiftly, checking corners, opening closets, peering behind stacks of canvases and crates. But there was no sign of anyone else in the building. She knew she should feel relieved about this; they'd interrupted the heist, and these maniacs had apparently not yet killed their victim. But something felt wrong. Something felt off.

As she was looking into a small closet that turned out to be a supply closet with cleaning supplies, she spotted a length of rope in the corner. She grabbed it and hurried back to the thief she'd bested. He'd managed to get his knees, which made it that much easier for Vivian to tur his wrist together, binding them behind his back.

"What about you?" she said. "Do you want to tell me where Andrea is?"

"Who?"

He looked confused…genuinely confused. Vivian felt herself losing her temper, her control beginning to wane. And as she stood up and headed back into the office with Sterling and the other thief, she once again focused on the fact that there were only two thieves here.

So where was the third who's been present at the Hankins residence earlier in the day? And wherever he might be, was Andrea with him?

CHAPTER TWENTY FOUR

Vivian could feel her fury boiling just beneath her skin. She couldn't recall the last time she'd been so angry. As she hauled the thief from the hallway into the office where the dagger had been held, everything started to feel smaller. The dimly lit office space felt suddenly claustrophobic, the air thick with tension and the musty scent of fear. In front of her, the two men shuffled uncomfortably, their eyes darting to each other, seeking some sort of silent reassurance. The one Sterling had shot was starting to go pale, the gunshot wound bleeding, though not profusely.

Sterling was on the phone when she ushered the other thief in, speaking to a cop or FBI agent nearby, requesting backup and an ambulance.

"Where is she?" Vivian's said, nearly roaring the question as Sterling's call came to an end. "Andrea—the woman from the art studio. What have you done with her?"

The thieves exchanged another glance, their confusion genuine—or expertly feigned. It didn't matter to Vivian; her patience had long evaporated. She lunged forward, a snarl contorting her usually composed features as she grabbed one—the leader, she thought, the one who's been shot—by the collar. She shook him hard enough to rattle his teeth.

"Talk!" she screamed, inches from his face. Her hands were shaking, but not from fear. It was anger—an all-consuming rage for the life hanging in the balance because of these men.

They both stammered, tripping over their words in their haste to deny any knowledge of Andrea. Their ignorance was like a slap in the face to Vivian, a personal affront to the unwritten code she had lived by as an art thief. You never involved innocents. You never crossed that line into violence. And now, her own rules made her complicit in this vile, trade-off—freedom for cooperation.

"We don't have any idea what the hell you're talking about!" pleaded the man who'd not been shot.

Sterling stepped in then, and Vivian could feel the calm radiating off of him. His tone was level, almost conversational, as if discussing the weather rather than the fates of these men. But there was an edge to it—a steel undercurrent that promised retribution.

"Let's be clear," he said, his British accent crisp and polite. "Eleven heists around the globe. Eleven women dead. We are quite sure that two of your associates are currently holding residence in interrogation rooms in an FBI field office here in the city. And you two *will* join them shortly. Without a deal, you're looking at life imprisonment, at best. And deepening on which country you end up imprisoned, the death penalty is on the table."

He paused, letting the weight of his words sink in before continuing.

"There were three of you when you hit the Hankins residence today," Vivian said, trying to feed off of Sterling's cool and calm demeanor "Where's the third?"

Vivian released her grip on the thief's collar, stepping back as Sterling took command of the interrogation. She watched the color drain from their faces, the stark reality of their situation finally dawning on them. There was no bluster now, no arrogance. Just the creeping dread of consequences they'd managed to outrun up until now.

"He's not here," the wounded one muttered, his voice barely above a whisper. "We don't know where he is."

Lies or truth, it didn't change the facts. The third man was out there, and Andrea's time was running out—if it hadn't already. Vivian felt the urgency clawing at her insides, the need to act, to find Andrea before it was too late.

"What's his name?" Sterling asked.

"Nightstar."

"His *real* name!"

The thief Vivian had fought in the hallway began to tremble a bit, and she felt like he might be on the verge of breaking entirely. She was quite sure this man was not the leader—the leader had likely been the wounded man, the one who'd come to the office to bust the safe.

"Daniel Marsh," the non-wounded thief said.

"Is he from overseas or a local like your two accomplices?" Sterling asked.

"He's from Essex."

"Shut the hell up!" the wounded one yelled. Vivian decided in that moment that he *was* the leader. And because 'Lionheart' sounded like a leader's name, she decided that's how she'd view him for now…even if it wasn't actually his codename.

"*You* shut up!" the cracking man said. "We're done now, *Lionheart!"* He spat the codename out as if mocking it, making fun of it. "Maybe if we help…"

"They won't take it easy on us," Lionheart said. "You know they won't…"

But a dam had broken in the other man, and it wasn't about to stop. "The other two…we don't know their real names. They were suggested to us as local checkpoints. We called them Jasmine and Gollum."

"Jasmine…that's Jenna," Sterling said. "She checked the places out before you came."

"Yeah, and she—"

"You can tell us all about that later," Vivian said. "For right now, we need to find Andrea. And if your third partner—this Nightstar—isn't here, do you think he has her?"

"Oh, for sure. He's…he's the one who always did the killing. The murders. But lately, think he got a little too wrapped up in it. He's different now...he's—"

"Do you have any idea why he didn't show up to help you tonight?"

"No. I think he got scared, He just…like I said, he's different now. He's far too invested in the murder part of it, and…and…"

"Why murder at all?" Sterling asked. "Why not just take the goods and leave?"

"That's how it started. But the first two jobs we did as a team together…there *were* legitimate witnesses. We kidnapped the first one—an older woman, about sixty or so. We weren't sure what to do with them. Nightstar was questioning her and…and he just snapped and killed the woman. A few days later, it was the same thing. These two drunk ladies were coming out of an apartment and just happened to see us. Nightstar…he didn't even think about it. he chased them down and killed them. We knew he was different then…"

"So why not just cut ties with him?" Vivian asked.

"Because our employer likes him. The guy is nuts and now has a taste for murder, apparently…like, *really* gruesome murders. And he's *really* good with complicated safes. Like creepy good, you know? So we just…we just let it go even though we told him time and time again, it was careless….that it would be easier for him to get caught."

"Where can we find him?" Sterling asked.

Before the thief could answer, the sound of approaching sirens reached their ears. Lionheart bristled a bit, grimacing at the sound.

"I... I don't know if—"

"Listen," Sterling interjected, his tone ice-cold yet clear. "The longer you take, the more danger she's in. You want that blood on your hands? One more body to add to your list?"

The question hung there, taunting, probing, piercing the veil of loyalty that had once bound Codex to his ominous comrade. Vivian watched, reading him like a telltale brushstroke on a counterfeit painting. Fear was their ally now, the final push needed to splinter the thief's crumbling loyalty to the murderous group he worked for.

“Some old, run-down motel. The Sunflower. That's all I know, I swear."

Vivian didn't waste a moment. She shared a terse nod with Sterling, a silent pact sealed between them. They were going after Nightstar, and they had to be swift.

Behind them, a voice called out from near the back door. “Agents? All clear?”

"We're good," Sterling said. "Come on in and take care of these guys, would you? We need to get a move on.”

Vivian looked out into the hallway and watched as a flood of blue uniforms and stern faces in FBI windbreakers poured in. Vivian barely noticed the agents taking their positions, securing the scene with practiced efficiency. Her mind was already miles away, racing alongside Sterling as they cut their way through the tide of bodies.

“You think we’re already to late?” Vivian asked as they ran across the wet sidewalk, then the street, toward their car.

“I hate to say it…but based on the way they’ve done things in the past, I’m afraid so.”

Vivian nodded, hoping that this detour in the groups usual set-up might be to their advantage—that because Nightstar had now taken this part of the equation into his own hands, they might still stand a chance.

And it was a hope she clung to desperately as Sterling brought the car to life and tore off into the rain-slicked night.

CHAPTER TWENTY FIVE

Vivian stepped over a puddle that reflected the neon sign flickering above the hotel entrance: *Sunflower* in lurid, orange letters. She pulled her jacket tighter around her, as much to ward off the chill of the rain as the seediness of the Midtown establishment. It was the kind of place you forgot by morning, but stuck to you like dried sweat at night.

Vivian and Sterling wasted no time, the car parked at a bit of an angle in one of the empty spots in front of the building. When Sterling opened the front door, he nearly slammed his shoulder into it in his haste. Inside, the lobby smelled of stale cigarette smoke and despair. A single light fixture buzzed overhead, casting a sickly yellow glow over the wallpaper. Vivian kept her eyes narrowed, alert for any sign of movement that didn't fit the slow rhythm of the place. She doubted a room here was very expensive and were used primarily for one-night stands, prostitution, and drug-related business deals.

Sterling led the way to the front desk, his posture rigid with purpose. The clerk, a waifish man with twitchy eyes, barely acknowledged them until Sterling produced his Interpol ID. "Daniel Marsh," he said, voice steady. "Which room?"

The clerk was momentarily frozen but nodded quickly as he typed something into his ancient laptop behind the desk. It took just ten seconds or so before he found what he was looking for.

"312," the clerk muttered, eyeing the badge again and then standing at his post importantly.

Sterling only gave the man a nod as they hurried off in the direction of the first-floor halls. There were no elevators in the place, so they made a direct line for the stairwell, situated in the middle of the hallway. They raced up the stairs, Sterling already drawing his holstered Glock. When they came to the third floor, Sterling's hand came down gently on Vivian's shoulder.

"You should stay here," he said, his eyes scanning her face for agreement. "You're unarmed and we don't know what to expect."

"Like hell I will," Vivian snapped, brushing him off. Her past life had taught her how to handle herself, with or without a weapon. "I'm not letting you face him alone. He's dangerous. And I have to…I have to see this through."

"Fine," Sterling conceded, his jaw set in a line that told Vivian he wasn't happy about it. "We don't have time to argue about it. But you *stay behind me."*

Together, they made their way done the hall with quiet steps. It came like second nature to Vivian but she was impressed how a man with Sterling's considerable bulk could move so gracefully. The threadbare carpet muffled their footsteps, which helped. The air was heavy with a cocktail of must and stale cigarettes. Each door they passed whispered secrets of the transgressions that hid behind them.

They came to room 312, and Vivian felt her blood go cold for a moment. Sterling gave her a quick glance as if to make sure she was ready for what might happen next. She nodded, and he sprang to action.

He didn't waste time knocking. Without hesitation, Sterling delivered a swift, decisive kick near the doorknob. The door flew open with a menacing crack, hinges groaning under the assault as the frame splintered. They stepped into the murky room; shadows clung to the corners like cobwebs. The place was a quiet, subtle mess. The untidy bed and scattered belongings painted a stark picture of someone on the run.

"Clear," Sterling mouthed, sweeping the main space, his body taut, ready for anything. But it was just the two of them in that moment—no sign of Daniel Marsh or Andrea.

"He's not here?" Vivian asked.

Sterling had moved to the only other space in the room, a small, dingy bathroom. It, too, was empty. "Doesn't seem like it," he said.

But just as he said this, a soft moan punctured the silence, drawing their eyes to the right. A thin door sat to the left, directly beside the very small dresser. Sterling moved first, one hand reaching for the knob, the other still holding his Glock. He turned the knob and pulled the door open. The sight that greeted them cleaved through Vivian's practiced composure.

Andrea was curled up like a discarded puppet, her red hair matted with blood, her skin marred by bruises and cuts. She was naked, and her eyes were wide with fear and pain. She mewled like an injured animal as Vivian and Sterling looked down at her.

The woman was alive, but barely clinging to consciousness.

“Andrea?” Vivian said, slowly getting to her knees to meet the woman’s eyes. “We’re here to help, okay. This is Agent Sterling, and my name is Vivian. Do you think you can get out of there?”

Andrea nodded, but started crying the moment Vivian reached out to her.

"Shh, you're safe now," Sterling soothed, gently lifting her into his arms. He stepped over to the bed behind them and stripped one of the blankets from it. He handed it to Andrea, making sure to keep his eyes averted from her naked state.

"Daniel Marsh," Vivian said. “Did he do all of this to you?”

She nodded her head. “Calls himself…Nightstar. He was…he…he’ll be back soon. He said if I left this room, he’d find me and kill me. he said…he said…”

“It’s okay,” Vivian said. “you’re safe now. Now…can you tell me how badly you’re hurt?”

“Don’t know. I think my wrist is b…b…broken. And there’s a cut on my back…”

“Can I see?” Vivian asked.

Wincing, Andrea leaned forward as she got to her feet and started wrapping the blanket around her body. When she turned, Vivian saw the cut on her back. It started on her lower back and nearly made it all the way down to her buttocks. It didn’t look too deep, but it was bleeding freely.

“You think there’s any chance the clerk has a med kit or something?” Vivian asked.

“Maybe you should go check,” Sterling said. “Andrea…are you okay with being alone in the room with me right now? I’d like to ask some questions while Vivian goes to get some things.”

Andrea thought about it for a moment but eventually nodded.

“Okay,” Vivian said. “I’ll be right back. You’ll be safe with Agent Sterling.”

Vivian exited the room, running down the hallway and back to the stairs. They'd found her. She was beaten and abused, and God only knew what else…but she was alive. They'd stopped the thieves *and* saved Andrea. She supposed this could be considered a massive win, and a—

Her thoughts halted as a man stepped up from the stairs and onto the third-floor hallway. Both she and the man stopped, her eyes locked onto the man's piercing blue ones. She’d never seen the man before but when his eyes darted over her shoulder and to the rooms beyond her, she knew all she needed to know.

"Daniel Marsh?" she said. "Nightstar?"

His eyes went wide, confirming her suspicions. He was holding a plastic bag emblazoned with a drug store logo. He looked harmless, a skinny man dressed in a black coat and jeans. And before Vivian was fully aware of what she was doing, she started moving toward him. She *almost* wanted the bastard to run. She wanted her adrenaline to be fully spiked when she got her hands on him.

With a sinister smile, Marsh's hand dipped toward his waistband. He still held the bag in his left hand as he pulled something from the waist of his pants. Vivian knew what it was before even seeing the glint of metal in the sickly hallway light. In the suffocating silence of the hallway, Vivian knew there was no time to think. She'd made her choice, her move—and now Marsh was making his.

Vivian's reflexes took over before Daniel Marsh could even fully grip the gun. She launched herself at him with a speed that belied her elegant frame, honed by years of navigating the razor's edge between theft and capture. She called out for Sterling as she did so, just a split second before her body collided with Marsh. She hit him hard in the stomach, and right away, she felt his fists coming down on her back. She had no idea where the gun was—if he'd dropped it or if it was still in his grip. All she knew was that as they hit the floor together, the narrow hallway became a cyclone of flailing limbs.

She managed to leverage herself on top of him, driving a knee into his ribs and her fist into his forearm. The forearm attack did cause him to release the gun, and she watched it tumble across the carpet. Marsh screamed beneath her as they grappled for dominance. Marsh was strong, but Vivian had a good deal of that bureau training under her belt.

Still, somehow, in all of his flailing, Marsh managed to connect his fist with her jaw. Her head snapped to the side, but she absorbed the blow, her adrenaline a buffer against the pain. She responded with a punch of her own, her wrist still aching from the punch she'd thrown at the antique store. It took Marsh right across the mouth. She followed up with a forearm smash to his nose.

It was a move that effectively ended the fight. He went limp for just a moment, allowing her to slide herself to the right and wrap him in a chokehold. The moment she had it locked in, she realized that Sterling was rushing toward her, summoned by her calling his name just seconds before.

His eyes took in the scene as he moved in to lend a hand with Marsh. But Vivian saw the look on his face—astonishment, victory…maybe a bit of surprise. As Vivian continued to cinch in her hold, Sterling was able to grab Marsh's writs and cuff him with a secondary set of cuffs he'd equipped himself with in the car. With the Handcuffs clicked into place, the struggle—and the case—came to an end.

"Good work," Sterling said, with a hint of admiration in his voice.

Vivian nodded, releasing her hold on Marsh. She realized that she'd cracked his nose open, and her right arm was slick with his blood. But she didn't care. She got to her feet and looked back to room 312, thinking only of Andrea.

Pushing Marsh against the wall, he said, "You may want to know that the rest of your group have been captured. All of this is over. And honestly, it's all because of you."

To Vivian's surprise, Marsh actually giggled about this. Blood cascaded down his face and he smiled, still looking in the direction of the room where he thought he'd managed to take Andrea prisoner.

"Fox, you want to go back and sit with Andrea?" Sterling asked. "I already called an ambulance for her, so we're just waiting."

She nodded, glad to have the opportunity to get away from Daniel Marsh. Yet, before she walked away, she glanced at Sterling and they smiled at one another. They'd managed to close the case and save a life, but something still felt incomplete, and Vivian couldn't tell what it was.

Though, as she started walking back to the room to sit with Andrea, it started to become clear.

Things felt unfinished because even after Andrea, there were still more lives to save…more criminals to stop. And though every fiber of her being fought against such a conclusion, Vivian couldn't ignore the fact that she'd not get the chance to save lives if she remained a thief.

The answer, of course, was simple. But it wasn't one she was ready to face just yet.

CHAPTER TWENTY SIX

From New York City, to Paris, to Lyon all in five days. It was dizzying, to say the least, and it was the chief reason that Vivian felt so damned tired when she arrived at the Interpol offices in Lyon just five days after wrestling down Daniel Marsh in a seedy hotel. Despite her weariness and the slight twinge if pain from a wrist that had indeed been fractured, the sunlight that streamed through the expansive glass façade of the Interpol building was warm and inviting as, casting a geometric dance of light and shadow upon the polished marble floor.

Stepping into this space made her adventure with Sterling back in New York feel like a lifetime ago, but the fractured wrist and permanent mental image of a beaten and bruised Andrea was enough of a tether to remind her that it had been much more recent.

With each step, her heels clicked assertively, a rhythm that seemed to echo the gravity of this moment. The receptionist, a young woman with an air of understated professionalism, glanced up from her computer screen and offered Vivian a cursory smile.

“Puis-je vous aider?” the woman said.

Vivian cringed, slightly embarrassed. "I speak *very little* French.”

The woman smiled and said, “No worries. Can I help you?”

“Vivian Fox…I’ve got a meeting with Director Garnett.”

“Ah, yes, of course. She’s expecting you! Come on…I’ll lead the way.”

The young woman led Vivian across the enormous lobby and to a set of wide steps that looked out along a glass wall to the right. At the top of the stairs, they tuned right down an impressive, wide hallway lined with doors. The receptionist led Vivian to the third door on the left and knocked.

“Here you are,” she said. “Have a good day.”

The receptionist turned on her heel and left, likely having no idea the amount of nerves and tension Vivian was feeling. Vivian reached for the doorknob but the door was opened before she could grab it. She *knew* it was Garnett’s office but still felt almost shocked to see her.

"Vivian, it’s so good to see you,” Director Elise Garnett said.

"Thanks. Much better here than in the back of a well-furnished prison van, right?"

The joke only got a brief chuckle as Garnett led Vivian into her office. The space was a testament to meticulous order—sleek and professional, with every book and file in its place. Director Garnett took a seat behind a large, modern desk made of dark wood, the clean lines of her office furniture reflecting the efficiency of her rank. Diplomas and commendations adorned the walls, interspersed with tasteful art that hinted at cultural sophistication.

"Have a seat," Garnett said, gesturing to the leather chair opposite her. Her eyes held a calculating gleam, assessing Vivian with a scrutiny that could unravel secrets. It had been Garnett who had requested this meeting just a single day after Vivian and Sterling had apprehended Daniel Marsh and brought an end to the entire group. And it was starting to really make Vivian nervous because she had no real idea what this meeting was about. For all she knew, she may still end up in prison for all of her past transgressions.

Vivian took the seat and waited. She didn't have to wait long because Garnett instantly began to talk. The woman seemed genuinely pleased to have Vivian in her office.

"Michael Sterling speaks highly of you, Vivian," she began, folding her hands atop the desk. "A job well done, he said. He's not one to hand out praise lightly. But he says you impressed him at every turn...though he could have gone without you charging at a man with a gun while you were unarmed."

Vivian nodded, unsure how to respond. Sterling's approval meant more than she cared to admit, a validation of her worth beyond the shadows of her past. It was a strange twist in the narrative she had written for herself.

"His words carry weight here," Garnett continued, her gaze never wavering. "And they've tipped the scales in your favor. Though, I like to think I may have also had a bit to do with that."

Vivian shifted in the leather chair, her fingers tracing the stitching along its armrests as Director Elise Garnett leaned back in her own seat. So far, things seemed to be going well, but Vivian still felt uneasy.

"Vivian, there's been considerable discussion about you at Interpol." Her eyes flickered momentarily to the digital clock on her desk, as if time itself were part of the negotiation. "And not just recently, because of this case. But as you know, your name has been circling around here for years as we tried to figure out ways to stop your…well, your *previous* career."

"Previous career?" Vivian said.

"Yes. Well, if that is what you choose. You see, given some of the more recent conversations concerning you…there is an offer on the table."

The air seemed to still around them, charged with the weight of what was to come. "What sort of offer?"

"An opportunity for a clean slate. However, should you decline, there will be... consequences." The threat, though veiled in professionalism, was palpable. "Remember, the first time you and I actually spoke face-to-face, I'd just had you captured in Charlottesville. We'd go back to that right away, and you'd spend time in jail. I'll level with you…not *much*, but still…I have a job to do, you understand."

"Yes, I understand." She inhaled sharply, a mixture of defiance and resignation tightening her chest. "It seems my choices are rather limited."

"Sterling insists you'd be a great addition. And based on the results I saw out of New York, I have to agree."

Vivian thought about what she'd felt as she'd walked back into the hotel room with Andrea—the feeling of things unfinished because of all of the other lives she could help to save. The choice, as it turned out, was an easy one.

"If I come aboard," Vivian said, "I'd like to ask one favor."

"Okay. what's the favor."

"I'd like to be able to look into a case. An old case that—"

"Your father's case." Garnett interjected.

Hearing it spoken so plainly made Vivian's heart skip a beat. Her father—and her sister—were part of her life that she rarely ever spoke of, something she kept in the dark. She'd *almost* mentioned it to Sterling but had rested on the rudimentary version of the story concerning the missing girl from her childhood neighborhood. *That* had been the driving reason she'd wanted to go into the FBI. But yes, proving that her father had been framed and maybe one day freeing him from a prison in France was now high on her radar.

That, and finding her sister.

"Yes," she finally said, feeling as if a ghost had just entered the room. "I'd like the freedom to look into my father's case."

Garnett frowned, though her foreknowledge of the story suggested that she had been expecting this. But the idea that Garnett knew of her deepest motivations without confession was a shining example of the woman's reach beyond these walls.. Vivian felt laid bare.

“Well?” she asked, unable to take the silence.

"*Unofficially*," Garnett stated, leaning in closer, "Interpol cannot direct resources to these... personal endeavors."

Vivian held Garnett's gaze, understanding the subtext. A nod from the director—barely perceptible—sealed their unspoken agreement.

"Unofficially," Vivian echoed.

“You still think he was innocent?”

“No. I…well, I don’t know.”

“Is that the only reason you’d take the job?”

“No.”

“I do know that you were on course to work with the FBI,” Garnett said. “Is your father’s path the reason you made such a drastic career change?”

"Partly." Vivian's admission hung between them. "At first, I wanted... something legitimate. To be on the other side of the law."

"Yet you ended up following in his footsteps," Elise observed. "An art thief…."

"His path had a certain allure," Vivian conceded, memories of heists and adrenaline flooding back. "But I need to know who set him up—who framed him."

“Does Sterling know about any of this?”

“No. And I’d like to keep it that way.”

Garnett smiled. “You know, it sounds like your decision has been made already.”

With her nerves on fire, Vivian nodded. “I suppose it has.”

“Good. Now, as I was saying, I can't task you with personal vendettas. But," she paused, locking eyes with Vivian, "should you choose to utilize Interpol's resources—discreetly, on your own time—I might just have other cases that require my undivided attention. Understand?”

The offer was a lifeline wrapped in barbed wire. Vivian's heart raced, her mind grappling with the gravity of the unspoken promise. To tread through her past with Interpol's power at her back was an opportunity she couldn’t pass up. Of course, she’d also have to *do the job* and have her own personal matters on the backburner.

"Yes, I understand," Vivian clarified, tasting the danger and freedom in the words.

Vivian felt the room close in around her, the weight of her choices pressing upon her. She could almost hear the ticking of the ornate clock on the wall, counting down the seconds of her old life.

"I need verbal confirmation, please," Garnett said.

Vivian pushed the words out, finding it a bit easier than she'd thought. "Yes. I accept your offer to officially work with Interpol."

"Good." Elise leaned back, satisfaction radiating from her. "Then let me offer you a fresh start. A very fresh start. Lyon, Brussels, San Salvador—you pick your stage, Vivian. We'll help you set up your new act."

The names of the cities echoed in Vivian's ears, each one a door to a different path. Lyon, the city that housed the very organization she was joining; Brussels, the heart of European politics; San Salvador, a canvas of vibrant colors and haunting shadows.

"Do I have to decide right now?"

"No. I'll give you a few days. In the meantime, you can work out of our offices here, knocking out paperwork and all of that."

"Okay…sounds good."

Garnett stood up, extending a hand across the sleek surface of her desk. "Congratulations, Agent Fox. Welcome to the other side."

Vivian took the offered hand, the handshake sealing her fate. It was official. She was part of Interpol now, an agent with a badge and a cause. Yet, beneath the surface, the rogue still stirred, not sure if she could leave that part of her life behind.

Agent Fix, she thought. *Damn, that does have a ring to it…*

It was foreign but not unwelcome. And the smile she and Director Garnett shared echoed with the promise of redemption and adventures—or perhaps, another splendid fall from grace.

NOW AVAILABLE!

ALL HE HIDES
(A Vivian Fox Suspense Thriller —Book Two)

As an art forger leaves a trail of deception and death through Europe's esteemed galleries, Vivian Fox—once the thief, now the tracker—must match wits with a killer who leaves no stroke uncalculated.

ALL HE HIDES (A Vivian Fox Suspense Thriller—Book 2) is the second novel in a new series by mystery and suspense author Ella Swift. The series begins with ALL HE TAKES (Book 1).

The Vivian Fox series will keep you on the edge of your seat with a gripping cat-and-mouse narrative brimming with chilling surprises and featuring a captivating yet haunted female protagonist. With constant suspense, action, and surprise twists, this series is sure to have you reading well past bedtime. Fans of Melinda Leigh, Kendra Elliot, and Lisa Regan are sure to fall in love.

Future books in the series are also available!

Ella Swift

Ella Swift is author of the VIVIAN FOX suspense thriller series, comprising five books (and counting); PEYTON RISK mystery series, comprising five books (and counting); and of the new COOPER TRACE mystery series, comprising five books (and counting).

An avid reader and lifelong fan of the mystery and thriller genres, Ella loves to hear from you, so please feel free to visit ellaswiftauthor.com to learn more and stay in touch.

BOOKS BY ELLA SWIFT

PEYTON RISK MYSTERY SERIES
WHAT'S HIS (Book #1)
WHAT'S LEFT (Book #2)
WHAT'S WISHED (Book #3)
WHAT'S GONE (Book #4)
WHAT'S MINE (Book #5)

COOPER TRACE MYSTERY SERIES
SHATTERED MIND (Book #1)
SHATTERED LIFE (Book #2)
SHATTERED HOPE (Book #3)
SHATTERED DREAM (Book #4)
SHATTERED FATE (Book #5)

VIVIAN FOX MYSTERY SERIES
ALL HE TAKES (Book #1)
ALL HE HIDES (Book #2)
ALL HE COVETS (Book #3)
ALL HE NEEDS (Book #4)
ALL HE DESTROYS (Book #5)

Made in the USA
Middletown, DE
01 August 2024

58373189R00092